CHIMP ESCAPE

Elizabeth Laird was born in New Zealand but when she was three the family moved to England. Since then she has travelled to the furthest corners of the world and has encountered all kinds of animals. On one adventure she became lost at night in a Kenyan game reserve, coming a little too close to an angry rhino and narrowly avoiding buffalo and elephants. Her experience of the wild animals of Africa has helped her write the *Wild Things* series.

She is the award-winning author of *Red Sky in the Morning*, *Kiss the Dust*, *Secret Friends* (shortlisted for the 1997 Carnegie Medal) and many other children's novels.

Elizabeth Laird has been helped in her research for *Wild Things* by Kenyan wildlife experts and ordinary country people, whose lives are constantly touched by the animals amongst which they live.

GW00801694

WILD THINGS

CHIMP ESCAPE

Elizabeth Laird

MACMILLAN CHILDREN'S BOOKS

Series consultant: Dr Shirley Strum
with the support of Dr David Western, past
director of the Kenya Wildlife Service

First published 2000 by Macmillan Children's Books
a division of Macmillan Publishers Limited
25 Eccleston Place, London SW1W 9NF
Basingstoke and Oxford
www.macmillan.co.uk

Associated companies throughout the world

ISBN 0 330 39380 4

A CIP catalogue record for this book is available from
the British Library.

Phototypeset by Intype London Ltd
Printed and bound in Great Britain by Mackays of Chatham plc, Kent

For Shaun, Craig and James

whose grandparents, Sheila and Dave Siddles, welcomed me warmly to their chimp refuge in Zambia. They introduced me to Stephan, Louise, Roxan, Barbie, ET, Sampie, Brian, Thomson, Clement, Doreen, Junior and a host of other chimps, who climbed all over me, untied my shoelaces, groomed my hair, hitched rides on my shoulders, turned out my pockets, and gave me enthusiastic hugs and kisses. I will never, never forget them.

ACKNOWLEDGEMENTS

Macmillan Children's Books and Elizabeth Laird would also like to thank Karl and Kathy Ammann, experts on chimpanzees and their plight today, and Charles Mayhew of the Tusk Trust, for their help in the research for this book.

For a long time, this had been a favourite place of the chimpanzees. There was a waterfall here, a clear cool spout that cascaded down a tumble of rocks to a pool below. Two giant fig trees grew up from the edge of the pool. Their massive, grey-pitted branches soared up towards the cloudless sky, and from them hung thick, rope-like lianas.

The chimpanzees had arrived here in the middle of the day. The crash of falling water and the clouds of spray excited the young males. They leaped onto the hanging lianas and swung out across the pool, yelling challenges to each other. Then they grabbed hold of branches and shook them violently, displaying their strength and courage. Birds took off, squawking in alarm at the noise. They wheeled up into the air and fluttered off to settle again out of harm's way.

The young chimpanzee mother, her infant clinging to her back, took refuge in one of the fig trees, climbing up to the highest branches where she could sit and feast peacefully on the sweet ripe figs. She settled herself, and her infant scrambled over her shoulder and tumbled into the safety of her lap. He took a long drink from her nipple, then leaned out over the crook of her knee to watch the antics of the males below.

His mother, grunting with enjoyment, reached out for another fig. She ate delicately, her strong lips working over the succulent flesh, allowing her baby from time to time to take morsels from her mouth.

Neither of them noticed the small figures creeping towards their tree. At the last moment, the baby's bright brown eyes caught the glint of light on a straight grey, hard-looking thing, that was slowly rising and pointing towards him. He watched it with innocent curiosity.

The gun's deafening report sent the chimpanzees fleeing in terror, but the infant's mother, toppling slowly off her branch, fell like a stone into the pool below. Her son fell with her, and as the cold water closed over his head, his old life disappeared forever.

Rough human hands grabbed him and pulled him out of the water. He was screaming with terror, crying for his mother. She had been dragged out of the water too, and lay on the ground, the blood pouring from a wound in her side. As she died, the men laughed and punched the air, delighted with the success of their hunt.

1

EMERGENCY LANDING

'Are you all right, dear?'

Mrs Hamble was sitting in the seat in front of Afra in the little thirteen-seater plane, and she had to twist round and raise her voice above the roar of the engine.

'I'm OK.' Afra managed to produce a brief smile. She didn't feel OK. The plane was bucking through the air pockets above the green forests of the Congo like a rodeo steer and her stomach was swooping and diving in nauseating lurches.

I'm not going to be sick, she told herself, feeling a cold sweat break out on her forehead. I'm just not.

She was hanging on to herself determinedly. This trip was going to be different from all the other times she'd been away from home. Neither her father, nor her foster-mother, nor her friends were with her today. She was flying alone, to a country she'd never visited before, to spend a week with her father's sophisticated French girl-friend. There were new clothes in her bag, and she had dared, that morning, to apply a touch of blusher to her cheeks. She had never felt so grown-up in her life.

Throwing up like some pathetic little kid will just ruin everything, she told herself, clenching the muscles of her stomach against the imminent threat.

She fastened her eyes on the ash-coloured curls that covered Mrs Hamble's head. They were quellingly prim and tidy, and not one hair strayed down onto the neat white collar of her faded print dress.

Afra looked away. The sight of Mrs Hamble's head was the last thing she needed right now. She had disliked the woman the moment she'd set eyes on her.

'Now don't worry about a thing, Professor Tovey,' Mrs Hamble had said, almost roguishly, to Afra's father, when he'd come to see the two of them off at the airport in Nairobi. 'I'll deliver your precious girl safe and sound at Luangwa. We'll be landing at a few places along the way, on mission business, but we'll be at Luangwa in time for tea. And your lady friend will be there to meet Afra?'

Prof had briefly closed his eyes, but had recovered enough to say, 'Minette Delarue, yes. She'll be at the airstrip.'

'What a lucky girl, Afra!' Mrs Hamble had cried. 'Flying all the way from Kenya to Zambia just to see some game! Maybe there'll be elephants. And lions! You'd like that, wouldn't you?'

Afra had stared at her incredulously.

'Elephants? You wouldn't exactly go to Zambia if you wanted to see elephants.'

'My, we do know a thing or two, don't we?' A hint of dryness had entered Mrs Hamble's voice. 'Well, elephants or no elephants, I'll make sure we get you all right and tight to your friend. It's not often that a mission plane makes a detour to a game park, but seeing how it's you, Professor Tovey . . .'

Her voice trailed away.

'It's very good of you,' Prof had said heartily, not meeting Afra's eye. 'I wish I could come with you myself. I have two more classes to teach this week, but—'

'But you'll be popping down to Luangwa at the weekend,' Mrs Hamble had finished for him, making it sound as if the flight halfway across Africa, over thousands of miles of forest, lake and savannah was as cosy as a visit to a sweet shop. 'Well now, we mustn't keep our pilot waiting. Time to say goodbye to Daddy, Afra.'

The memory of this awful conversation had diverted Afra's attention from her stomach, and she realized, with pleasurable surprise, that the flight had settled down to a normal smoothness. She looked sideways at the occupant of the single seat across the aisle. An African boy, somewhat

5

older than herself, was sitting there. His eyes had been shut, but he opened them, as if aware that he was being scrutinized, and turned to look at Afra. His hands had been clenched on his knees, but now he turned them over and spread out his fingers.

'I think you were afraid,' he said, 'just now, when the plane was going like this.' He made dipping motions with his hands.

'Afraid? Of course I wasn't.' Afra's eyebrows met in a sharp frown.

The boy's smile faded a little.

'I'm Mwape,' he said, introducing himself.

'I'm Afra.' She turned away from him and tucked a wayward curl behind her ear. 'Did you say Mwape? I don't know that name.'

'It's a Zambian name. Why should you know it?' he said, a little grandly.

Afra bridled.

'I'm half-African. And I can speak Swahili.'

'We don't speak Swahili much in Zambia. My tribe is Bemba. Mwape is a Bemba name.'

'Oh.' She had never heard of the Bemba people but didn't want to admit it.

'Where are you going?' Mwape went on after a short silence. 'Does your mother work in the mission?'

'My mother?' Afra was puzzled for a moment, then saw that he had glanced at Mrs Hamble. '*She*'s not my mother. My mother was Ethiopian.

She died years ago. And I'm going to Luangwa, in Zambia, to the famous game park there.' She paused. 'It's like a bus, this little plane, isn't it? It stops off all over Africa. I mean, we started this morning in Kenya, and hopped over Uganda, and now we're somewhere in Congo, I suppose. And I'm getting out in Zambia. Where are you stopping?'

'Lubumbashi,' Mwape said. 'It's in the south of Congo, right beside the Zambian border.'

'I thought you said you were from Zambia?'

'I am, but my father works in a hospital in Lubumbashi. He's a doctor. That's why I'm on this plane. He sent me up to Nairobi to deliver some blood samples.'

Afra looked at him, impressed. Mwape smiled at her a little condescendingly.

'You don't look old enough to do that kind of thing,' Afra said crushingly. 'Don't you go to school?'

'I'm fifteen. Nearly. And it's holiday time now. Look at you. You're not at school either. Why are you going to Luangwa?'

Afra was about to tell him about Minette, her father's girlfriend, who was making a business trip to the famous Zambian game park and had arranged for Afra to meet her there, but the words were squeezed out of her as the little plane was suddenly buffeted by a violent gust of wind.

She looked out of the window. Mountainous

7

indigo clouds were racing towards them. In a moment they would be engulfed.

'A storm!' she shouted at Mwape. 'Look!'

The other passengers, two young American women and five African men, were fumbling at their waists, checking that their seat belts were properly fastened. Mrs Hamble turned her head.

'Don't worry, lovey. It's just a little storm. We're safe in God's hands, don't forget.'

She didn't have time for more. The storm struck the plane with full force. Afra felt it judder beneath her, as if it had been hit by a powerful jet of water, as if it was being tossed about on a boiling, turbulent river. Then, with terrifying suddenness, it tilted sideways and began to drop, falling, plummeting, like a shot bird out of the sky.

Afra felt her mouth open. A scream would have emerged from it if her breath had not been squeezed out of her body. They were plunging downwards so fast that only her seat belt was preventing her from slamming against the roof of the plane.

She heard, as if from a great distance, one of the women in the front of the plane moaning aloud, 'Oh God, no, oh God, please.' She hardly noticed that Mwape's hand had shot out across the aisle and that he was gripping hers so hard that her fingers were almost cracking.

Then, when she expected at any moment to hit

the ground and die, the plane miraculously came out of its dive and began to climb. It was staggering drunkenly, buffeted from side to side by the vicious blows of the hurricane force wind.

Mwape dropped her hand. Afra nursed it in the other, uncramping her crushed fingers. Sobs were rising in her chest, suffocating in her throat and emerging as whimpers.

We'll drop again. We'll dive and hit the ground. We're going to die. We're going to be killed now, she thought, the words running round and round in her brain. She had forgotten about being grown-up. She felt like a frightened baby, wanting an adult to pick her up and make her feel safe again.

Mrs Hamble's head had disappeared and Afra knew that it would be bowed down in her hands.

She's praying, she thought. Pray for me too, Mrs Hamble. You'd better say one for me.

She couldn't pray herself.

The plane's engine roared with a new ferocity as it lurched through the rain, which was now lashing against the fuselage.

The door at the front of the cabin suddenly burst open. Afra could see the cockpit, and the back of the pilot's seat. His brilliantly white shirt stood out against the black clouds beyond the windscreen. His straining shoulders were pushed back against his seat as if he was pulling on something with all his might. The plane was still climbing steadily. The sight of the big man at the controls, his bare mahogany-coloured arms seeming to bear up the plane under his own strength, was briefly comforting.

A flicker of yellow sparked against the windscreen and crackled past her window as a bolt of lightning struck the plane. Afra couldn't see the co-pilot, but she heard his voice, which wafted back to the terrified passengers as he shouted, 'It's hit the GPS! We've lost our avionics!'

Afra didn't understand the words but they struck fresh terror into her heart. As if she sensed her fear, Mrs Hamble turned round. Her lips were trembling a little, but her face was almost surreally serene.

'Don't worry, Afra. I told you. We're in His hands.'

'Didn't you hear him? The other pilot?' Afra's voice was tight with tension. Mrs Hamble's calmness seemed so weird it was almost more frightening than fear would have been.

'The navigation instruments have stopped working, that's all,' Mrs Hamble said. 'The Global Positioning System. From the satellite. It's all right. I know Peter Mpundi. He's a very good pilot. I taught him when he was in eighth grade. He'll find his way safely, like they used to in the old days, with maps. There's nothing wrong with the plane. My word, that was a nasty bump we had back there, wasn't it?'

'A nasty bump?' repeated Afra, trying not to sound hysterical. The plane had been crashing to the ground, they were all about to die, her heart had left her body, Mwape had nearly finished off her right hand for good, and Mrs Hamble called it *a nasty bump*?

Mrs Hamble was still looking at her, the corners of her pale eyes wrinkled with concern.

'Would you like a boiled sweet, dear? It helps with airsickness, I find.'

'No, thank you,' said Afra faintly. She'd forgotten her nausea. Fear had driven it away. Mrs Hamble retrieved the book which had flown off her lap when the plane had dived and settled her glasses back on her nose. Afra stared at the unruffled curls on the back of her head with old hostility mixed with new respect. Either Mrs Hamble was so dumb she honestly hadn't realized they'd all just survived a deadly peril, or else she had so much faith she just knew she could persuade God to bring them out of it safely.

I guess it must be the faith thing, she thought, feeling humbled.

The plane was steadier now, as if it had responded to Mrs Hamble's calmness. Afra looked sideways at Mwape. He was wiping beads of sweat off his forehead. He looked shaken.

'Did you mind that I held your hand?' he said. 'I thought you might be afraid, and if you are afraid it is good to have someone to hold your hand.'

She looked at him, her eyes narrow.

'Afraid? I was totally out of my head. But you were too. I saw your face. And anyway, you were squeezing my hand so tight you nearly broke every single finger.'

He grinned.

'Did I hurt you? I am sorry. My father says I do not know my own strength.'

'Go on, admit it.' She felt a little resentful. 'You were pretty scared too.'

He put his hands up.

'OK. A bit. I was a bit afraid. But it was exciting! To have some danger, it makes you feel, I don't know, it makes you feel more alive.'

'Just before you die, you mean.'

'Yes. I mean no. You cannot always just be safe. That is so boring. Think about James Bond. Jackie Chan! Arnold Schwarzenegger!'

Afra rolled her eyes.

'Oh boy. I hope you never learn to fly a plane. If you do, I'll make sure I'm not on it. Hey, look. The clouds have gone. The sun's out again.'

'It is now.' Mwape looked out of his side of the plane. 'But there is another storm coming. Look.'

She leaned over the aisle to look past him. A new bank of clouds was erupting over the horizon, purple, grey and black billows piling up into the sky. Ahead, she could hear the co-pilot's voice again.

'Correct. Requesting emergency landing at Mumbasa. Storm damage to our avionics. We'll never make it to Lubumbashi before the next big one. Over.'

Then, as if he had suddenly realized that the cockpit door was open, the co-pilot's hand shot out, hooked itself round the edge of the door and pulled it shut.

'Where's Mumbasa? Where are we?' Afra asked Mwape.

'It's a little town, in a kind of forest area. I was there once with my father. The loggers are there.'

'Loggers?'

'The people who are cutting the forest.'

Afra looked out of the window. The plane was flying low. Below her she could see the great forest stretching out to the horizon. The crowns of the trees looked soft from above, like cushions of bright green moss.

They're not soft though, Afra thought. There are hard tree trunks and spiky branches and stuff down there. You crash into that and you don't have a chance.

She tried to imagine the forest, the green light filtering through the great trees, their canopies alive with birds and butterflies, and the damp earth below, over whose soft surface elephants might still roam, and antelopes, and warthogs, and a thousand other creatures.

And there'll be monkeys, all kinds of them, she thought. Chimps maybe. Gorillas, even.

She focused her eyes, as if by trying she could overcome the distance and penetrate the green carpet to see the mysteries below. Then, emerging from beneath the plane, she saw a long red gash running through the forest.

A road, I guess, she thought. It looks kind of odd. Like a wound or something.

The plane was banking steeply, losing altitude so quickly that the trees seemed to rush up to meet it. Afra's stomach tightened with fright again.

'We're coming into land,' Mrs Hamble called out over her shoulder. 'Soon be there. Just a little diversion at Mumbasa. Don't worry. We'll get you to Luangwa, Afra dear.'

Afra could see that they were circling round over a small town whose houses were clustered in a clearing of the forest. Clouds had scudded in again, and rain was once more drumming on the windows. The airstrip was in view now, a stripe of red through the green that ran, improbably steeply, up the side of a hill.

We can't land here! Afra thought, panic rising in her again. We'll never make it!

The wind had taken hold once more, and the little plane was being tossed about like a shuttlecock. Afra squeezed her eyes shut, screwing up her mouth and nose as if tensing them for the impact she felt certain would come. But then, suddenly, a more familiar bump, a welcome shudder, jolted through the plane, and her eyes flew open. The wheels had touched down on the gravel strip. They were back on good firm ground.

Her heart rose in a welling up of relief and delight.

'We made it!' she said, turning to Mwape with a huge grin, as familiarly as if she had known him for years.

'Yes, thank God,' he said.

'To Him be praise indeed,' said Mrs Hamble primly, turning to offer them both a triumphant smile.

2
MUMBASA

Afra's legs felt shaky when she stepped out of the plane. In spite of the rain that was cascading out of the sky, the heavy heat wrapped itself around her like a blanket. She ran after Mwape, whose long legs were fast covering the muddy ground that lay between the little plane and the shed-like airstrip building.

They ran in through the door at the same time, and she realized that he was taller than she had thought. He towered over her, and though his long arms and legs were still coltish with recent growth, he looked much older than fourteen.

He grinned at her.

'We are wetter than fish,' he said.

Mrs Hamble splashed after them into the make-shift building, which was so small that the seven other passengers it already contained made it feel crowded. She was holding her bag above her head in a vain effort to keep her head dry.

'Soaked to the skin!' she said, with a bright smile. 'Lovely weather for ducks.'

Afra moved across to the rain-streaked window and looked out. She could see the pilot, sheltering under a wing of the plane, in conversation with another man, who was pointing up to the wing and shaking his head. The two broke out and ran towards the building. The pilot arrived first. He shook the rain out of his eyes as he came inside.

'I'm sorry,' he said, addressing the passengers. 'A problem has developed with the flaps, due to storm damage. They can't fix it until the rain stops. Also, our navigation systems must be repaired before we can fly on to Lubumbashi.'

The passengers started talking loudly to each other in a variety of languages. Captain Mpundi held up his hand.

'I'm sorry,' he said again. 'We can't go on today. We will have to stay the night here in Mumbasa. Transport is already on its way from the town. It will take you all to the mission hostel. There is room there for everyone.'

'Oh! Oh dear!' For once, Mrs Hamble looked disconcerted. 'How am I going to contact Luangwa, Afra, to tell them you're delayed?'

'Can't they radio Luangwa from here?' said Afra. Her heart had sunk at the thought of spending the rest of the afternoon, the whole evening and part of tomorrow with Mrs Hamble, using up these few precious days of her half-term holiday when she could have been exploring the delights of Luangwa with Minette.

Mrs Hamble's trill of laughter broke in on her thoughts.

'Now why didn't I think of that? It takes a young brain, I suppose.'

An old vehicle, half-minibus, half-station wagon, was already pulling up outside. The passengers, hesitating on the threshold, made a dash for it through the rain, cramming themselves into the little space and steaming up the windows almost at once.

Afra found herself squashed onto a seat between Mwape and Mrs Hamble, and the minibus took off at speed, careering over the bumps and through the puddles, making its occupants grunt and squeal.

The rain had stopped by the time they had covered the mile or so from the airstrip to the town of Mumbasa, and Afra shook out her dark curls in the steaming still air as she stepped out of the minibus and looked around.

She wasn't used to the thick succulent growth and the lush greens of this tropical Africa. Her Africa, her home in Kenya, had the fresh tang of high altitude, where the air was cool and the trees and bushes and flowers softer, fluffier somehow, than all this strident growth.

It looks like a monkeyish, leopardy kind of place, she thought, looking across to the edge of the forest, whose huge trees seemed to erupt almost violently from the wet red earth behind the long low mission buildings. She could see flashes of coloured feathers among the leaves, even from here, and hear squawks and flutings from tribes of semi-invisible birds.

This is it, she told herself. It must be. The great forest of Central Africa.

A shiver of excitement ran through her. She was standing on the edge of a vast jungle, one of the wildest places still left on earth, and its green shady depths held secrets as yet hidden from humankind. There were plants here that no one had ever discovered, whole species of insects unknown to scientists, and even strange birds and animals, no doubt, whose existence had never been suspected.

I want to explore it all, thought Afra, but then she shook her head. No I don't. It's too scary.

It wasn't the animals that scared her here, but the militias of armed soldiers, who were active everywhere in this war-torn country, where civil war had been raging for years.

'Afra! Over here, dear! Your room's over here.'

Mrs Hamble was waving at her from one of the smaller buildings, a long row of rooms with a veranda running along in front of them.

It took Afra only a few minutes to inspect her sparsely furnished but scrupulously clean little bedroom, and to unpack a few things from her bag. She looked at her watch. It was still only early afternoon. There was nothing to do for the rest of the day.

She wandered outside again. Mrs Hamble was emerging from the main building.

'They're radioing now,' she called out, her voice sounding tired. 'They're trying to contact Luangwa. It'll take a while, I shouldn't wonder. Now you're not to worry about a little bitsy thing. Everything's going to be just . . .'

Her voice tailed off and she put a hand up to her head. 'Oh dearie me. One of my heads coming on again. I'll have to lie down at once.' She pressed both palms against her temples and looked across at Afra. 'There are books in the sitting room. Just ask for . . . They'll get you some tea around . . . Oh my. This is a bad migraine. It was that terrible flight that brought this on.'

She's human then, Afra thought, with guilty triumph, but when she saw how pale Mrs Hamble was, and how she stumbled as she walked along the path towards the row of bedrooms, she felt sorry for her after all.

The rest of the afternoon and evening stretched achingly ahead. The books in the sitting room didn't sound very interesting, but there was nothing else to do. Afra began to walk across to the main building. Mwape was coming out of it. Behind him, she could hear the crackle of a radio transmitter.

'They can't get through to Luangwa,' he said. 'Now they are trying to call my father in Lubumbashi. He will pass on the message for you.'

'Oh. OK.'

Luangwa and Lubumbashi seemed unreal and far away. Getting messages through didn't seem to matter somehow.

'I'm going to walk into town,' Mwape said. 'It's not far. Do you want to come?'

'Yes!' Afra said eagerly. 'There's nothing to do here, and Mrs Hamble has gone to bed with a migraine. Wait. I'll get my sunhat.'

The mission compound was on the edge of the township of Mumbasa, and the unmade-up road outside the gates was wet and slicked with sticky mud. Afra stepped over the first puddle and jumped back, startled. A cloud of butterflies, which had been resting on the edge of the water, fluttered up like a puff of feathers. There were little blue ones, big white ones, and swallowtails with black and green streaked wings. They fluttered round Afra, their delicate wings almost stroking her bare arms.

'Oh, how lovely! They're so lovely!' she cried, delighted.

Mwape was already striding on. Gently disengaging two brown and orange butterflies that were clinging to her T-shirt, Afra hurried after him.

The first buildings of Mumbasa were in view now. They were small huts, covered all over with broad palm leaves. As they came closer, Afra could see an old woman, wearing a skirt made of long yellow grass, sitting outside the hut. She stood up, and Afra saw that she was tiny, no taller than Afra's shoulder.

Afra tried not to stare at her, but then a young woman came out of the hut, with a boy behind her. They were very small too.

Mwape looked down at her, amused.

'You have not seen pygmy people before?' he said. 'They live in the forest, deep inside it. They are very clever at hunting, and you can see, they are very small.'

Pygmies! thought Afra. She had heard of pygmies, of course, the fabled small people who lived in the great forest and knew its secrets like no one else.

'I just didn't realize they were so – well, so small,' she said lamely.

A pygmy child ran up to her, and reached up to tug at her hand. She grinned at him, and blew out her cheeks to make him laugh. He ran away, squealing with a mixture of delight and alarm.

A little further on were some more substantial buildings, roofed with corrugated iron. The first was a little shop.

'Maybe I should get something for Mrs Hamble, since she's feeling so bad,' she said reluctantly, 'only I don't know what to get her.'

'But you don't have Congolese money, do you?' said Mwape.

Afra looked relieved.

'No, but I have some dollars. Everyone takes dollars. But it doesn't look as if there's much to buy here.'

The little shop's shelves were crowded with dusty old tins and bottles. There were boxes of matches, some candles, some bright pink soap and a few packets of flour, rice and pasta. Mwape had spotted some biscuits on a low shelf, and he was pointing them out to the man behind the counter. Afra turned away and looked along the road as she waited for him to buy them.

There were only a few people around. A couple of old men, too tall to be pygmies, were squatting in the shade of a tree, and three young women were walking down the road in single file, baskets filled with vegetables balanced on their heads. A few metres away a balding pygmy wearing a blue-checked shirt was talking to a much older man. The tall man held a gun in his hands and as Afra watched he passed it to the pygmy and said something in a language Afra couldn't understand.

Mwape had finished buying his biscuits, and he was watching the two men too.

'Chimpanzee,' he said suddenly, pleased with himself.

'What do you mean?' said Afra, looking round. 'I don't see any chimpanzees.'

'The tall guy, just there, he said "chimpanzee".

I understood the word. I don't know their language, but I recognized that word.'

The tall man put the gun into the pygmy's hands and they walked off in different directions.

'Why's he giving him a gun?' Afra said puzzled. 'Is it legal here? I mean, having guns like that?'

Mwape shrugged.

'No, but who is going to say anything?' he said. 'Maybe these men are hunters. The government does not care about hunters.'

'Hunters? And they were talking about chimps?' Afra was aghast. 'You don't mean – surely, you can't mean – that they're going to shoot *chimps*?'

Mwape was about to answer her when the roar of a heavy engine silenced him. A huge truck was approaching along the dirt road that ran out of the forest and into the middle of the little town. Afra stepped back as far as she could to let it pass, afraid of being splashed by the muddy water.

The driver's cab was high above the powerful engine, and behind it a massive trailer carried three huge tree trunks. Dying orchids and ferns, that had once sprouted from their moist bark, still clung to them. The truck drew to a halt and the African driver opened the cab door and climbed out. His passenger, a thick-set European man with a stubble of close-cropped blond hair all over his head, clambered out after him, and strode towards the little shop.

Afra, her eyes wandering idly along the length of the truck, stiffened and grabbed Mwape's arm.

'It can't be!' she said. 'There! Tied to the log, at the back. It looks like – a gorilla, or a chimp or something, and it's dead!'

3

A HORRIBLE TRADE

Afra ran up to the back of the lorry to look more closely at the grisly thing that was lashed to one of the tree trunks, but before she reached it, she faltered. The sight was too horrible to bear. In one swift glance, she took in a mass of black hair, clotted with blood, a lolling hand, and a face from which sightless eyes stared out with awful blankness. She wanted to be sick, and turned away.

The European man was coming towards her. He seemed concerned about one of the truck's wheels, and bent down to look at it.

'*Du*, Maurice!' he called out. '*Komm mal*. Look at this.'

His voice was heavily accented.

Another European, a little shorter and lighter, jumped down from the truck's cab.

'*Ecoute*, Dieter,' he said with irritation. 'Always you make a big noise over nothing. That wheel, I told you before, there is no problem.'

'Excuse me.' Afra had plucked up her courage, and now she approached the two men. 'What happened to the chimp?'

'What chimp?' said the big man.

'He's there, tied to the back of your truck. He's dead.'

'It's not a "he". I'm sure it is a female,' the small man said. 'The baby was still with her.'

'A baby? She had a baby too?' Afra said, her throat tightening. 'Was there an accident or something?'

The two men looked at her, surprised. Dieter, the bigger one, snorted with laughter.

'Accident? How can you shoot a chimp by accident? They are damn difficult to hit, you can believe me.'

'You mean you *shot* her? You killed her *deliberately*?'

In spite of the clammy heat, Afra felt an ice-cold shiver run down her back.

The big man was staring at her belligerently.

'You think I have time to go hunting? Who are you? What are you doing here?'

'What does it matter?' Afra was glaring at him, the ice in her body turning to red heat. 'Who killed her then, if you didn't?'

The smaller man laughed.

'*Ma pauvre petite*,' he said. 'Don't you know what happens around here? That is not a chimpanzee there now. It is meat. Only meat, nothing more. Do not upset yourself.'

'Meat?' cried Afra. 'Meat? You mean you're going to *eat* her?'

Maurice shrugged.

'For myself, no. I do not like the meat of the chimpanzee. But many people in the city, in Kisangani or in Isiro, they find it is very delicious.'

'But they're – you can't – chimps are practically human! Anyway, they're a protected species!' Afra's voice sounded even in her own ears like a childish wail, and she tried hard to control it. She had to stay in command of herself. Nothing would be gained by losing her temper.

The big man was still looking at her, anger and suspicion in his eyes.

'*Ach, scheisse*! Tell her to get lost, Maurice. Do you want more trouble, or not?'

A small crowd of onlookers had collected – a few men, who had just emerged from a bar, and some children in school uniform, who were carrying books under their arms. On the edge of the crowd, the same height as the children, were several pygmy men. One of them, the balding man in the blue checked shirt, was still carrying the gun.

Maurice gave Afra an avuncular smile.

'This is not your business,' he said. 'These people,' – he indicated the crowd with a sweep of his hand – 'all of them, they are not shocked. Do they look surprised to see a dead chimp? No! For them it is something normal. For them, hunting chimps, it is for their income, for money, to feed their families. Do you want these kids to be hungry?'

Afra heard someone behind her take a deep breath and clear his throat. She turned round and saw Mwape stepping forward to stand beside her.

'It is not normal to me, no,' he said. He was frowning fiercely. 'To kill chimpanzees, it is against the law.'

'The law! What law? Who is interested in the law?' scoffed Dieter, while Maurice, with a shrug, pointed to a policeman who had appeared on the other side of the road and who was greeting the truck driver with a cheerful, prolonged hand-shake two metres away from the dead chimp.

Afra moved a little closer to Mwape, grateful for his support. She felt shaken and confused. The big man's acrid sweat was in her nostrils, and his lowering presence intimidated her, while the smaller man's patronizing voice was rubbing at her outraged feelings like sandpaper on a wound.

'I think you're disgusting,' she said, unable to control the tremor in her low, tight voice. 'You're butchers. You're sick.'

Both men burst out laughing.

'We are butchers, we are sick and disgusting,' said Dieter. 'The little girl does not like us. I am so scared!'

'If you do not like us, *mademoiselle*, we will take ourselves away,' said Maurice. 'I told you

29

Dieter, there is nothing wrong with the wheel. *Allons-y.*'

The crowd began to move away.

'Where is Clement?' Dieter said, looking round with irritation. 'That driver, he is never here when we need him.'

He scrambled up into the cab of the truck, and sounded a deafening blast on the horn.

The driver had been taking a cardboard carton out of the cab and had carried it into the shop. He came running out again with a banknote in his hand. He stuffed it into his pocket and vaulted up into the driver's seat.

'*Au revoir, ma petite*,' Maurice said to Afra, smiling at her in an amused way that made her want to stamp her foot and scream at him. 'Little girls are always sentimental. It is sweet to be like you. Unfortunately, you will grow out of it.'

He disappeared round to the far side of the truck, and Afra heard the passenger door open and close. A moment later, a cloud of grey exhaust belched out from the back, and the truck moved off down the road. The body of the dead chimp jerked pitifully as the wheels bumped over the uneven surface, and Afra closed her eyes and turned away, unable to bear the sight any longer.

'Who are you?' a new voice at her elbow said. 'Do you know these men?'

She opened her eyes. A tall young African in a yellow bush shirt was frowning down at them.

'No. I just met them,' she said, 'and I hope I never see them again as long as I live.'

'Who are they?' Mwape said, his voice indignant. 'What is happening?'

The man in the yellow bush shirt studied him for a moment, his eyes wary.

'There is a very bad situation,' he said at last. 'Do you really want to know about it?'

'Yes!' Afra and Mwape spoke together.

'You are strangers here, I think,' the young man said, a touch of bitterness in his voice. 'You see things from the outside. I will tell you, if you like, but not here. Here, there are too many people. Where are you staying?'

'At the mission hostel,' said Afra.

'I will walk back there with you,' the young man said.

He set off, and the other two fell in beside him. Afra was burning to ask questions. She could feel an awful sorrow building up inside her, and knew that if she was not careful it would erupt in a lava flow of anger. She tried to concentrate, to push her feelings down and frame questions in her head.

'Why—' she began.

The young man held up his hand.

'Wait,' he said. 'It is better to talk when we are private.'

They walked fast, both Mwape and the young man having to hurry to keep up with Afra, who was almost running in her burning impatience. She halted suddenly, outside the gates of the compound, and they almost bumped into her. She was looking down at the puddle where, half an hour earlier, the butterflies had flocked. The wheels of the logging truck had smashed through it, turning it into a deep rut, and several crushed butterflies, their wings no more than fragments now, were stuck to the muddy edges.

Tight-lipped, Afra led the way into the mission compound, and the others followed her to a spreading tree, in whose shade a few chairs stood round a metal table. They all sat down.

Afra opened her mouth to speak, but the young man was staring down at his hands as if he was thinking, and she waited, her own hands gripping each other under the table.

'I am Manou, Daniel Manou,' he said at last. 'I am the conservation and wildlife official for this region of Congo.'

'Conservation and wildlife official?' Afra burst out. 'That's so great. Oh, we're so lucky that we met you. You're the very person who's dealing with all this! You're going to prosecute these guys, right? Make sure—'

'Please! You must wait and listen to me,' Daniel said, tapping the table with his forefinger.

He paused.

He doesn't know what to say, thought Afra, doubts beginning to rise. Maybe he isn't planning on doing anything. Maybe he's just going to let those people, those *monsters*—

Daniel broke in on her thoughts.

'Where are you from?' he asked, looking at them in turn. 'Why are you here? Is there an adult with you?'

'We were on a flight from Nairobi to Lubumbashi today,' Mwape explained. 'We're travelling alone. Not together, I mean.'

Daniel looked enquiringly at Afra.

'I'm supposed to be with Mrs Hamble, but you can't count her. I'm on my own too, really. I'm going on to Luangwa.' There was a tinge of pride in her voice. 'We shouldn't be here at all, but there was a storm.'

'I know.' Daniel nodded. 'It was a very violent one here too.'

'The plane made an emergency landing,' Mwape went on. 'It is a little damaged, so we can't take off until tomorrow.'

'You came from Nairobi? Then you are from Kenya?' Daniel said.

'I am,' said Afra.

'I am Zambian,' said Mwape, 'but I live in Congo, in Lubumbashi.'

Daniel took a moment to absorb this complicated information. Then he said, 'You do not know then, what is happening here, in the forests?'

Both Mwape and Afra shook their heads.

'It is a very bad thing, bad for the forests, and the people and especially for the animals.' Daniel rubbed one hand over his eyes as if he was tired. In the tree overhead, a large black hornbill landed with a noisy flap of its black wings, braying out a hoarse cry, but none of the three at the table glanced up at it.

'The logging companies have been in other parts of Congo for a long time, and now they have arrived here, in Mumbasa,' Daniel went on. 'They are from Europe, from France, Germany, Switzerland, I don't know where. They are taking our hard wood away to make furniture for the gardens for people in Europe. They are driving roads deep into the heart of the forest, and cutting down the biggest trees to export.'

'I thought you couldn't do that,' objected Afra. 'I thought the forest was protected.'

'It is, some of it,' said Daniel. 'They are allowed only to take certain trees. Usually, they do this correctly. In this area, at least, I can make sure of that.'

'But where do the chimps come into it?' demanded Afra.

'To get into the deep forest, the loggers have to make roads, like the road here. It is a good opportunity for businessmen. People in the cities, they like to eat meat, rare meat, meat from the forest. Duiker, bush pig, chimp, gorilla –

especially chimp and gorilla. They say it is very delicious.'

A shudder of disgust ran through Afra.

'I don't believe I'm hearing this,' she said.

'The businessmen,' Daniel went on, ignoring her, 'they employ the pygmies, who are very clever at hunting, to shoot the animals for them.'

'Oh,' said Afra, remembering the pygmy with the blue shirt. 'I saw – never mind. Go on.'

'The pygmies have always hunted for themselves,' Daniel went on. 'They would catch a mouse deer or an antelope, or some small animal when they needed meat to feed their families. They used only nets, or bows and arrows. Never guns. Sometimes they killed chimps, but not so often, and they were never a danger to the wild animals. They lived beside them. The duiker and the bush pig, they were afraid of the man. The man, he was afraid of the leopard and the elephant. That is the life of the forest.'

'The natural life,' Mwape said, nodding.

'Yes, the natural life. But these businessmen, they have changed everything! They are giving guns to the pygmies. Wherever the loggers' roads go, they go. "Kill all the animals you can find", they say to the pygmies. "We will give you money, and you can buy beer and clothes and cigarettes." The pygmies have no other way to get the things they like, so they take the guns and hunt. The businessmen cheat them so much! They give them a few coins only, and when they sell the meat they make a big profit.'

'But it's *illegal*! It must be!' said Afra, the blood rushing to her face.

Daniel spread out his hands.

'It is illegal, yes. But what can you do? Did you see the policeman, standing there? He saw the dead chimp. He knows what is happening. I have spoken to him so many times! But the loggers pay him something, and he says nothing. He has a family too, and his salary is low. The money is necessary to him.' He sighed. 'It is so bad now. They are killing so many chimps, and gorillas too, that if we do not stop it soon there will none left. They will be wiped off the face of the earth.'

Afra seethed in silence. She was biting her lips so hard they hurt.

'But the foreigners, the logging companies, why don't they do something?' said Mwape. 'It is their fault, after all. They could refuse to allow the meat merchants to use their roads. They could at least stop carrying meat on their trucks.'

'Oh, the loggers!' Daniel laughed bitterly. 'You saw those men. What do they care? This is not their country, their forest, their animals. They are here only to make money, to grab what they can and run home with their riches to Europe. Yes, they could stop all this trade, but they refuse. I have tried to tell them, but they only laugh at me.' He paused. 'I hate this work. It is not a good job for me. What can I do here? I am applying for a transfer to another government department.'

Afra could hold herself in no longer.

'They're thieves! Murderers!' she cried, her voice rising. 'I want to – I'd like to see one of *them* bouncing around on the end of a log, like that poor chimp. I can't bear it! Daniel, what can we do? What are we going to *do*?'

4

THE BABY IN THE BOX

'We can do nothing!' Daniel sat back in his chair, lifting both palms in a gesture of resignation. 'I have tried my best. I have thought of many things, but it is no good. Everyone wants only one thing. Money. The loggers, the businessmen, the pygmies – all they want is money.'

The three of them sat in a depressed silence for a moment. They were so still that a pair of tinkerbirds ran down the trunk of the tree and hopped onto the table, crying 'Tink-tink-tink-tink!' like a pair of alarm clocks running down.

Mwape was the first to move. Alarmed, the tinkerbirds fluttered off.

'I am going to get some tea for us,' he said. 'We have to cheer ourselves up. And we can eat my biscuits. Oh!'

'What's biting you, Mwape?' said Afra.

'My biscuits! I left them at the shop. I forgot to bring them back with me.'

'Let's walk back into town then,' said Afra, jumping up. 'Anything's better than sitting here, like three miserable old depressives, for the rest of the day. Anyway, Prof – he's my dad – he says that walking sometimes helps you to get ideas.'

They went out into the road again and turned back towards the town. They didn't speak much this time.

Think. You have to think of something, Afra kept telling herself, but her mind remained an obstinate blank.

Daniel stopped before they reached the shop, to talk to a pygmy friend.

'I'll catch you up,' he said.

There was a crowd outside the shop, and as Afra approached them, a little ahead of the others, she could see that they were mainly children. They were clustered round something on the ground, peering down at it, then jumping back and shrieking with alarm and excitement.

Mwape overtook Afra, and pushed through the children to get to the shop door, then he saw what they were doing and stopped so suddenly that Afra, who was close behind him, ran straight into him. She bent her head sideways to look past his broad back, and gasped.

A cardboard carton lay on the ground in the centre of a small group of children. It had obviously contained tins of soup at one time as the word *Campbell's* was printed on the side. In it cowered a little chimp. He was lying curled up, one black-haired arm hugging himself, as if he was trying to seek comfort. He was looking up at the crowd of children with terror in his round brown eyes, and his lips were pulled back from his teeth in a grin of fear.

The biggest boy, showing off to his friends, crouched down, and poked the little chimp under his bare pink ear. The baby whimpered and turned his head.

Afra shot forward as if she had been stung.

'Stop! Are you crazy? You heartless little beast. Leave him alone!' she yelled.

Mwape said nothing, but he leant forward and swiped at the boy, shoving him back, away from the box. The boy fell over onto the ground and said something angrily in a language Afra couldn't understand. The other children moved back, muttering and frowning.

Afra snatched up the box and cradled it in her arms. Her hand accidentally brushed the chimp's skinny elbow, which was sticking out of the box, and he flinched, cringing away from her, trying to make himself as small as possible.

'What are you doing? Put that box down,' said an angry voice in Swahili behind Afra's shoulder.

She turned to see the shopkeeper coming out of the shop.

'That chimp's mine,' he went on. 'You can't just pick him up and take him. I paid good money for him.'

'You bought him just now?' Afra was trying to keep her voice down, and to sound polite. 'But he's only a baby. He's too young to leave his mother, isn't he?'

The shopkeeper shrugged.

'His mother's dead.'

'Oh!' Afra remembered the box the driver had carried into the shop. 'Then that other chimp, the dead one – this is her baby?'

The shopkeeper frowned.

'How do I know what happened to its mother? I paid for it, I tell you. If you want it for a pet, you'll have to give me a good price.'

'How much?' said Afra.

She knew, even as she said it, there would be a heap of trouble ahead. She heard Mwape drawing in his breath beside her. She shut out the sound. She would think of the consequences later. She knew only that she had to rescue this baby from his tormentors.

'Twenty dollars,' said the shopkeeper.

'Twenty dollars? US dollars?' Mwape gasped. 'That's too much. Don't give it to him, Afra. Not more than ten.'

Afra placed the box carefully in Mwape's arms and felt for the money-belt at her waist.

'I'm not going to bargain,' she said disdainfully. 'You can't bargain for a life.'

She pulled out a twenty-dollar bill and handed it to the shopkeeper.

'But what are you going to do with him?'

An anxious frown was creasing Mwape's

forehead. Afra nearly smiled. She had seen the same expression many times on the faces of her two best friends, Tom and Joseph. Every time, in fact, that she'd lost her head and run slap into an animal rescue mission.

'I don't know what I'm going to do,' she confessed. 'We'll have to think about it.'

Mwape didn't notice the 'we', as Tom or Joseph most certainly would have done.

'But he needs food,' he went on, looking at Afra as if she was crazy. 'You don't know what he eats.'

'You're right,' Afra said briskly. 'He certainly needs to eat. Milk, that's the best thing. He's only a baby, and babies need milk. I fed my bushbaby and my puppy on milk, and they did OK.' She stepped over the threshold after the shopkeeper, who had retreated into his shop and was putting the twenty-dollar bill into his drawer. 'Please,' she said, trying to keep her temper. 'I need a baby's bottle, and a teat, and a tin of dried milk powder.'

The shopkeeper grinned.

'That'll be forty dollars,' he said.

'That's not fair!' snapped Afra. 'You cheated me over his life, but don't think you can do it again.'

The shopkeeper frowned.

'You think you're a smart one,' he said. 'Does your mother know you're buying a pet chimpanzee for yourself?'

'My mother's dead,' said Afra curtly. 'Like this baby's.'

The shopkeeper, taken aback by the ferocity in her face, backed away from her. He took a tin of milk powder off the shelf, fished under the counter for a bottle and a teat, and handed them to her.

'I don't have any Congolese money,' Afra said, handing him another dollar bill.

The man took some change out of his drawer and gave it to her.

'I gave you a fair price,' he said sourly. 'Tell that to your moth— your father. And tell him to teach his daughter some respect for her elders. I didn't cheat you. Chimps are getting rarer round here. The prices are going up.'

Afra had turned away and was leaving the shop, suddenly desperate to get the baby to a quiet place where she could prepare his bottle and feed him.

'Look after it!' the shopkeeper called out after her. 'They eat what humans eat at that age. You have to feed them all the time. And watch out in case it bites you. They're very strong, even when they're so small.'

The children were crowding round the entrance to the shop, staring at Afra and trying to get a last glimpse of the chimp. Mwape strode through them, clearing a path for her.

Daniel was still talking to his friend. When he

saw Afra and Mwape coming, he bent down to shake the man's hand in farewell.

'What have you got there?' he said, looking into the box, and exclaiming with astonishment as he saw the baby chimp, who was shivering with fear, huddling against the cardboard in a pathetic attempt to feel more secure. 'What happened? Where did you get this?'

'He's that poor chimp's baby,' said Afra, through gritted teeth. 'The one we saw on the truck. Those – those monsters sold him to the shopkeeper. I just bought him.'

'You bought him?' Daniel sounded annoyed.

Afra didn't answer. She was already hurrying back down the road towards the mission hostel, anxious to escape from the buzzing crowd of children that were following close behind her.

'But you're going on to Luangwa,' said Daniel, speeding to keep up with her. 'How do you propose to take him there?'

'In the plane, with me,' said Afra, who had no idea.

'Oh really? Don't you know it is illegal to take chimps out of Congo? I can't possibly allow this. Even if I let you, you would be stopped at the border.'

'Is it illegal? No, I didn't know.' Afra hardly heard him. Her whole being was concentrated on the pathetic little creature in the box, whose cries had weakened to feeble whimpers.

You'll die if I don't feed you soon, she thought. Hang in there, baby. We'll soon be home.

'This is very bad,' Daniel was saying impatiently. 'You cannot just buy a chimpanzee. Even if you get permission to export it, what would your family say?'

'I'm not going to take him home with me,' said Afra. 'I'm going to let him go in the forest in Lubumbashi. Lubumbashi's still in Congo. Nobody could object to that.'

Daniel shook his head and clicked his teeth angrily.

'There is no forest like this one at Lubumbashi,' Mwape said. 'It's all acacia trees, small trees only, and not at all like the forest here. It is not good for chimps at Lubumbashi.'

'Oh.' Unconsciously, Afra was slowing down. 'Well . . .'

'You must give him to me,' Daniel said, holding out his hands. 'I will send him to the zoo at Kisangani.'

'A zoo? Never!' Afra's hands tightened round the box. She had seen monkeys and chimps in cages before. They had sat listlessly, rocking backwards and forwards on the bare concrete, holding on to the bars and stretching out their hands to passers-by.

'Then I will find a nice family, good people, where he can live,' Daniel said.

Afra hesitated.

'If I give him to you, would you release him into the forest here, when he's strong enough?' she said hopefully.

'No. What are you thinking of? Don't you know anything? He is too young to survive without his mother. He won't even know what foods he can eat. He will never adapt to the wild way of living. Anyway, after he has been with humans for a time he will lose his fear and come too close to them. He will be caught again very soon, and shot.'

Afra felt like crying with frustration. With an effort, she said lightly, 'I guess we'll have to sort it out later. The first thing is to get some milk into him. Just look at him. I bet he hadn't had as much as a sip of water for hours and hours, and nothing to eat since he lost his mom.'

They had reached the gates of the mission compound. Daniel stopped.

'I have work to do now, but I will return later,' he said, his voice severe. 'I will find a solution for the baby, and tell you of my decision.'

'Thank you,' said Mwape, who was beginning to look harassed.

'Thanks,' Afra called out over her shoulder. She summoned up a smile and tried to look grateful and child-like. She wanted to keep him away as long as she could. She had thought he would be an ally but he seemed more like an enemy now, another obstacle to work round.

She had already gone through the gates and was making for the table under the tree. Tenderly, she lowered the box down onto it.

'It's OK, little one,' she said softly.

She longed to reach out her finger and stroke the little black hand that was clinging tightly to the edge of the box, but she held back. It was too soon to touch him. She would have to work for the privilege, to wait, to gain his trust.

'Mwape, could you stay with him for a little while till I get some water to make up his feed?' she said. 'Oh boy, just look at him. We're going to have a hard job to set him to rights. He is one sick, sad little chimpanzee.'

5

A BOTTLE OF MILK

Afra was used to making up milk feeds for
orphaned babies. She'd fed her own bushbaby
that way, as well as countless other small creatures that had found their way into her hands and
out again into the wild. She mixed the milk
quickly with water from the bathroom, and was
back a few moments later with the full bottle in
her hands.

She returned to find Mwape standing some distance from the table, talking to a man in a
battered straw hat, who was leaning on a scythe.

'He's the gardener,' Mwape told her in English,
knowing the man wouldn't understand. 'I am
keeping him away from the table. It is better if
no one knows. They will only ask too many questions, and try to take him away.'

He spoke with relish, enjoying the idea of a
conspiracy.

Afra flashed him a grateful smile.

'Keep him busy while I get the baby into my
room. Then come on over. We have to talk.'

She picked the box up and, holding it carefully,
walked off, leaving Mwape to nod patiently while

the gardener, who was delighted to have a captive listener for once, tipped his straw hat back on his head and started on another long tale.

Afra opened her bedroom door with a shiver of relief. No one had seen her. She put the box down on the bed, and, very gently and slowly, lowered the teat of the milk bottle towards the listless baby's long brown lips.

'I want to pick you up so much,' she murmured, hoping her quiet voice would soothe him, 'but I guess you've been thrown around enough already. Look, baby, this is milk. There's milk for you here. No, don't close your eyes. It's OK. I promise I'm not going to touch you. I'm going to wait till you want to touch me. It's going to be your choice.'

The baby's head was still turned away, and his eyes were closed. He seemed to be retreating into himself, shutting out the terrifying world into which he had suddenly been catapulted out of the familiar embrace of his mother and his family in the forest.

'You have to drink,' Afra went on, carefully modulating her voice so its calm sound would reassure him. 'If you don't take something soon, you'll die. Do you know that?'

She lowered the teat still further till it was gently touching the baby's upper lip. He opened his eyes and looked up at her sideways, but his mouth remained firmly closed.

A muffled cough from somewhere nearby made Afra jump, and a drop of milk fell between the baby's lips. Afra looked over her shoulder. No one was outside the window. The coughing came again.

It must be Mrs Hamble, she thought. Her room's next to mine. I'd better take care, or she'll hear me.

She turned back to the baby. He was licking the milk off his lips and eyes were fully open. He was gazing up at her with the wide, staring scrutiny of the very young.

'Yes,' she whispered. 'It's good, isn't it?'

She pressed the teat between her thumb and finger and a little more milk dribbled into his now half-open mouth. He turned it round with his tongue, as if unsure of the strange taste, then pushed his lips out a little.

'More?' whispered Afra. 'That's right. You like it, don't you?'

Gently, she stroked his half-open mouth with the teat, watching a few drops of milk roll out of the corner and spill onto the sparse dark hair of his chest, but the baby was turning his head now, beginning to feel for the teat with his lips, which were forming themselves into an exploratory O. Then suddenly, he seemed to make up his mind, drew the teat firmly into his mouth and began to suck. The small black hairless hand, which had been clutching convulsively at the side of the box, relaxed, and he laid it across his skinny, hairy belly. His eyelids drooped a little, and his eyes became hazy with pleasure.

Afra heard a discreet tap at the door, and without taking her eyes off the baby called out softly, 'Come in.'

Mwape shut the door behind him and came to stand beside her.

'That gardener, he was going to talk for ever,' he began, in a normal voice.

'Shh!' Afra gave him a warning look. 'Mrs Hamble's in the next room. I heard her cough just now.'

The baby's eyes had shot open when he had heard Mwape's voice, and his hand had grasped the side of the box again. He stopped sucking and looked up at Mwape, who put out a hand to tickle his tummy.

'No,' Afra said sharply. 'Not yet. He's not ready to be touched yet.'

'How do you know?'

Mwape sounded offended.

'It's kind of – you see, I've brought up a whole heap of orphans,' Afra said placatingly. She didn't want to upset Mwape. She needed him on her side. 'Little animals, birds, a puppy. You just learn to get inside their heads. I mean, this little guy has been grabbed at and pushed and thrown around by heaven knows how many strangers these last few days. I guess he needs a little time. Some space.'

Mwape sat down gingerly on the bed beside the box.

'OK,' he said, speaking quietly now. 'So you are going to make him your pet? You are going to keep him?'

Afra shook her head impatiently.

'No! I don't know. It wouldn't work out, where I live. I mean, first of all, how would I smuggle him into Kenya? My dad would never allow me to keep a chimp in Nairobi. And anyway, he'd need all kinds of stuff I couldn't give him. Lots of room to move around in, somewhere secure where no one could get hold of him, other chimps to be with – oh, so many things. Hey, I haven't had time to think about it yet. I guess we'll have to do one thing at a time. Right now I have to get some food into him, so he'll make it through today.'

'He will make it, all right,' Mwape said. 'Look at him. He has nearly finished all the milk.'

The baby had been sucking more and more greedily, and now he lifted his head in an effort to squeeze more out of the fast-emptying bottle. He finished the last few drops and pulled for a moment or two on the empty teat before realizing that he was sucking on air. Reluctantly, he let it go.

'He's so funny, like a baby, a human baby,' said

Mwape. 'That is what my little brother used to do.'

Afra pulled the teat out of the chimp's mouth.

'I know. Except that he's not. Human, I mean. It's going to be kind of hard to remember. I was talking to him when you came in a coochie-coo kind of a voice, and if I'd stopped to listen to myself – No, baby. Don't reach for it. It's empty. That's good now. You finished the whole lot. That's the first step. You're on the way.' She stopped, and smiled at herself. 'There I go again.'

The milk seemed to have given the little animal a spurt of confidence. He sat up for the first time and put one exploratory finger, edged with a hard black nail, over the side of the box to touch the cotton counterpane on the bed. Then he withdrew it, picked up his foot and began to examine the sole, dabbing at the lined bare skin with his fingers as if he was feeling for something.

'Must be a cut there or something,' said Afra. 'Let me look.'

Without touching the baby, she bent over, twisting her head round to examine the small black foot, whose toes, which were almost as long and agile as fingers, were curled over round the sole.

'Why, there's a huge horrible splinter stuck in there,' she said. 'Wait now, while I get it out.'

Deftly, she pinched the end of the splinter between her thumb and finger and extracted it with one quick movement. The baby hooted softly, and opened his mouth as if he was going to scream, then closed it, and began regarding Afra again, his huge amber eyes round with concentration.

Something caught in the back of Afra's throat. It was a kind of love, fierce and protective.

'No,' she said aloud, a little more forcefully than she had intended.

'What do you mean, "no"?' asked Mwape.

'He's not going to – I'm not going to let Daniel or anyone else take him away.'

She was going to say more, but then she stopped. Someone was running along the veranda towards the door of her room. A voice called out, 'Are you in there?'

She ran to the door and opened it, standing in the doorway to prevent whoever was outside from looking in. A man stood on the threshold, and she recognized one of the passengers from the plane.

'You have to come at once,' he said. 'They've fixed the plane quicker than the pilot expected. There are still a few hours of daylight. He wants to leave right now. He's planning to get as far as Lubumbashi tonight. I'm rounding everyone up.'

'Now?' Afra stared at him.

'Yes. The bus leaves in a few minutes. Which room is your mother in?'

'She's not my—' Afra began automatically, then

thought better of embarking on a long explanation. 'She's next door to me.'

'OK. You'd better be quick.' The man was already moving on. 'The pilot won't wait.'

Afra shut the door behind her and turned to look at Mwape, her face set.

'Well?' she said. 'Are you going to help me?'

Mwape looked wary.

'Help you? What do you mean?'

Afra clicked her tongue impatiently.

'Are you going to help me give him some kind of a chance, or do you want me to leave him for Daniel to get hold of, so he'll end up behind bars in a zoo, or on the end of a chain in some fat cat's backyard?'

'What do you want me to do?' He was frowning.

'I don't know!' Afra was chopping the air with her hands. 'I don't know what to do! But we can't just leave him here, can we, Mwape? You do see that, don't you?'

'But we can't take him with us! What can we do with a chimpanzee in Lubumbashi? I am going home. I think I can see my father's face, when I take a chimpanzee with me! And you are going to Zambia. Didn't you hear Daniel? It is illegal to take chimps out of Congo. They will stop you at the border.'

She felt like stamping her foot.

'Is that all you can say?' she burst out. 'Can't,

55

don't, won't! If we take him with us we'll at least have time to think, to make a plan.'

Inspiration struck her.

'I thought you liked danger and adventure,' she said. 'James Bond? Jackie Chan? They wouldn't even stop to think about it. They'd just smuggle him onto the plane and work out some brilliant plan, and—'

'Yes!' Her ruse had worked better than she'd expected and his eyes were dancing. 'And Jackie Chan would kick-box all the bad guys and do one of those rooftop escapes. You know. Jumping over gaps. To defy death!'

She couldn't help cutting him down to size again.

'In Mumbasa? I didn't see any two-storey buildings, never mind any skyscrapers.'

She was about to go on, but stopped herself. She didn't want to put him off.

The chimp suddenly yawned, exhaling his breath with a sigh that ended on a grunt.

They both turned and looked at him. He was sitting up in his box, scratching the top of his head with one hand, and holding his sore foot with the other. He looked so absorbed and so comical that they both broke into muffled laughter.

'No, we can't leave him,' Mwape said. 'That means that logically we have to take him with us.' His voice was quivering with excitement.

'That's right. It's the only thing we can do. But how the heck are we going to do it?'

'How? In his box.' Mwape was biting his lips, thinking and talking at the same time. 'We must cover it over with something.' He scanned the few items that Afra had pulled out of her bag and scattered at the end of her bed. 'Your towel!'

'Cover the box with my towel? But it'll just fall off. And he'll grab at it.'

'We'll tie it on.' Mwape was gaining confidence. 'Do you have any scissors?'

'Yes, in my sponge bag. Oh, I see. You mean we need to cut air holes for him in the cardboard so he can breathe.'

'No, I was thinking we could cut some strips out of something to tie round the edge of the box. So the towel will stay in place. But air holes are a good idea too.'

Afra was already fishing round in her sponge bag for her scissors. She pulled them out and began to cut a hole in the cardboard, working carefully and quietly so as not to alarm the baby more than she had to. He backed away from the strange sharp implement, drawing back his lips and cowering again against the cardboard, though less fearfully than before. When she had finished, to her relief, he lay down in the box and curled up like a puppy in a basket.

'I guess you're tired out,' muttered Afra. 'And now you're full of milk, maybe you'll just go to sleep. That's the best thing. Go to sleep, little guy. Here goes the towel over the box. Don't fret now.'

She laid the towel carefully over the box and waited anxiously in case the baby would react and tear it away, but he seemed to accept it, and apart from a little shifting noise and a quiet snuffle, remained still and quiet. She turned away and yanked something red out of her bag. Hesitating, she held the scissors above it.

'What's that?' asked Mwape.

'My new dress. It's the only thing I have that's long enough.' Afra looked at it unhappily for a moment, then lowered the scissors towards the soft material.

'No, wait.' Mwape looked scandalized. 'Don't spoil it. I'll fetch my bag. I have an old shirt. It is torn anyway. I don't need it any more.'

He ran out of the room. Afra quickly stuffed her other things into her bag, and from the bottle of drinking water that had been placed beside her bed, made up another feed of milk. To her relief, the chimp was quiet and motionless.

Think of a good story to explain where the box came from, she told herself. I can just hear Mrs Hamble. 'Why, Afra dear, whatever have you got in that funny old box? Are you going to let me peek?' She had been waggling her head, imitating Mrs Hamble's tiresome voice under her breath, but stopped, embarrassed, as Mwape burst back into her room, afraid that he had heard her.

'The minibus is here,' he said. 'Everyone is getting into it. Quick, we have to go!'

Afra's heart was pumping uncomfortably hard as she followed Mwape out of her room and walked across the small compound of the mission hostel towards the minibus. She was holding the box as carefully as she could, so as not to jolt and scare the baby into making a noise, or pulling at the towel. Mwape carried her bag.

Afra scanned the inside of the minibus. It was already half-full of passengers. They had become friends during the adventures of the day, and were talking and laughing loudly together.

She climbed into the bus and sat down by a window. Mwape sat beside her, and turned his back on her, twisting round, shielding her from the sight of the others with his body. Afra could see that he was enjoying himself.

It's just a game to him, she thought. But what if he decides to stop playing? I'll be stuck then.

Mrs Hamble was the last to arrive. She tottered across the compound, holding onto the arm of someone from the hostel's main building. Her eyes were puffy and her face yellowish grey. She looked into the bus, saw that Afra was safely on board, then sat down in the seat behind Afra and pressed her handkerchief to the side of her head.

Afra felt obliged to say something.

'Are you OK, Mrs Hamble?' she asked, twisting her head round carefully so as not to disturb the chimp. 'Is your headache any better?'

Mrs Hamble managed to produce a fleeting smile.

'It's just a migraine,' she said in a flat voice. 'It goes on for a while. I'll be all right soon.'

In spite of herself, Afra was impressed. Mrs Hamble was obviously feeling awful, but she wasn't going to make a fuss or hold anyone up. Guiltily, Afra felt grateful to the migraine too. She could have trotted onto the bus with a cheetah at her heels and a parrot on her shoulder and Mrs Hamble wouldn't even have blinked.

She had reckoned, though, without the two American women.

'Well, hey,' one of them said, turning round from the seat in front. 'What have you kids been doing? What's in the mysterious box, honey?'

Afra's heart lurched.

'Fruit,' she managed to say through a constricted throat. 'Bananas and – and stuff. Mwape and I went into town. We bought them there.'

'Fruit? But why the towel?' the other woman said, staring with interest at the bizarrely wrapped box. 'Looks like you have a wild animal in that thing. There weren't any tarantulas or cobras in with that batch of bananas, by any chance?'

She laughed comfortably at her own joke.

'The fruit is very ripe,' Mwape said, joining in enthusiastically. 'The bananas are fragile, you know? She is trying to keep the sun off them. Just to prevent them from going brown.'

The women's eyebrows rose, and more questions were clearly on the way, but at that moment the driver let the handbrake off and the minibus started to move, turning out of the gate of the compound and heading away from the town towards the airstrip. Afra sat back and let out her breath. She needed Mwape, but he was alarmingly unpredictable.

'Look there,' Mwape said in a jubilant voice. 'We have just passed Daniel.'

Afra looked back. Daniel was standing by the gates of the mission compound, looking after the minibus with irritation and disappointment on his face.

'I bet he was on his way to take the little guy,' Afra whispered. 'We got out just in time.'

For a second she felt regretful. Daniel would have taken the problem out of their hands. He would have provided a sensible, adult solution, and he would have appeased them with promises of the baby chimp's future happiness.

It wouldn't have worked though, thought Afra.

The baby would have ended up in a zoo, or with some horrible private owner, for sure.

It was too late to give the baby to Daniel, anyway. They were in for it now. There was no going back. The chimp was her responsibility, and somehow she would have to sort out a decent future for him.

Anyway, thought Afra, I don't regret a thing. I'm going to fight for this baby.

It was easier at the airstrip than she had feared. The pilot was already at the controls of the little plane and the co-pilot was standing at the door, urging everyone to hurry on board. No one took any notice of Afra and her box.

'Is this crazy,' one of the American women said to the other, 'or is it just plain suicidal? I mean, we hit a hurricane this morning, so what's the betting we get a tornado this afternoon?'

The co-pilot overheard.

'No, no,' he said soothingly. 'The weather is fine now. Look at the sky! Not one cloud upon the horizon.'

Afra and Mwape moved quickly to the back of the plane. There was only one seat on each side of the aisle and no one else wanted to sit so far back. Empty places divided them from the other passengers. Mrs Hamble hobbled on board last, and collapsed thankfully into the seat nearest the door, which the others had kindly left for her.

The door was closed, everyone strapped

themselves in, and the plane began to roar down the runway. For a moment, Afra forgot the little animal in the box on her knee, as fright gripped her stomach. What if that woman had been right? What if a tornado did hit them? The sky looked clear enough now. The sun was slipping down out of the deep blue vault of late afternoon towards a ridge of purple hills on the far horizon. As the plane rose higher she could see the forest stretching, green and dense, in all directions. It looked serene enough, but this morning the storm had rolled up out of nowhere. Couldn't another one do the same?

She didn't want to think about it. Instead, she concentrated on the rich green crowns of the trees below. Only this morning, she had tried to imagine the animals that lived down there in the moist, shadowy depths, and now, by a quirk of fate, one of the forest-dwellers was here, right here on her lap, depending on her for his whole future.

She could see the loggers' roads clearly now. They struck through the forest in long raw lines of destruction. Beside them were lighter green patches, places where the trees had been felled, perhaps, and new shrubby growth had sprouted up.

That's your home down there, baby, she thought, and they're destroying it.

As if he'd heard her voice, the baby chimp

moved. Afra felt his weight shift on her knees, and a scrabbling sound as his nails scraped on the cardboard. Then a round bump appeared under the towel. He was trying to sit up.

She looked across at Mwape. He was staring at the box, horror in his face, as if he had only just realized the enormity of what they had done.

'He's hungry again,' he whispered. 'Give him some more milk. Quick.'

He passed Afra the bottle from her bag. Gingerly, she released one corner of the towel from the strip of shirt that was tying it down. At once, a little hand appeared in the opening. Before she knew what was happening, an arm followed it, then a shoulder, and a moment later the baby had climbed right out of the box.

Afra heard a smothered gasp from Mwape, and she threw a worried glance down the plane. It was lucky that she and Mwape were sitting at the very back, with several empty rows between them and the nearest passengers. Everyone else was looking forwards, or sideways out of their little windows. Some had their heads back, resting against their seats, as if they were sleeping.

There was an awful picture in her mind of an excited chimp, loose in this confined space. Everyone would be terrified. They'd shout and lunge for him, and he'd panic, and bite them, and scream. And if he got into the cockpit, and started grabbing at the controls . . .

Her blood ran cold at the thought.

She needn't have worried. The chimp was still too weak from hunger and exhaustion to move away from her lap. He put up his long hairy arms and wrapped them round her neck, and his legs stole around her waist. Then he snuggled his head under her chin and lay cuddled against her chest.

Love surged through Afra, softening her muscles and making her catch her breath. Gently, she put her arms round the baby, holding him lightly but firmly, as she imagined his mother would have done. She breathed the warm smell, a mixture of hay and fruit and clean earth, that rose from his hunched shoulders and round head.

She stared down at him. His ears, bare of the black hair that covered the rest of his head, were round, and stuck out from his head like twin saucers. Blue veins pulsed under the coffee-brown skin. She couldn't see his eyes. A thick ridge of bone stuck out from his forehead, shading them from view.

Gingerly, she began to stroke the baby's rounded shoulders. The skin under the stiff hair felt firm, harder than a human skin. He seemed to sigh with contentment, and looked up at her, then he picked up her hand, put two of her fingers in his mouth, and began to suck them.

She wanted to cry.

'I love you,' she whispered. 'I only met you today, but I really, really do.'

Maybe this is how mothers feel with their babies, she thought. My mom never had a chance to feel anything for me.

The little chimp shifted, and she felt his hard bony bottom dig into her knee. It jerked her out of the wave of sorrow and love that was threatening to overwhelm her.

'But I'm not your mom,' she murmured, pulling herself together. 'And we have to be so careful. We're both in trouble here.'

She looked up again to check on the other passengers. No one had turned round yet. She pulled the scarf out of the bottom of the box and draped it over her shoulder. It didn't do much to disguise the baby, but it helped a bit.

Mwape touched her arm.

'Why are you waiting? Feed him quickly and get him back to sleep.' His voice was tense.

He'll be in worse trouble than me if we're caught, Afra thought guiltily. He lives here. His dad works at the mission hospital.

With one hand, she fished for the bottle that had slipped down the side of her seat and put it to the little chimp's mouth. He grabbed at it eagerly, and began to suck, and she shifted him so that he lay like a baby in her arms.

He gazed up into her eyes. He looked childlike but ancient at the same time, contented, but wistful.

But you must never think you know what an

animal is really feeling, Afra told herself. That's kind of a conceited thing to do.

He was sucking voraciously, and she was afraid he would splutter and choke. She withdrew the bottle a little, to give him a chance to breathe, but he pulled it out of her hands and thrust it back into his mouth.

'I don't know what we're going to do with you,' she murmured. 'This is one crazy thing I've got myself into here. I just have no idea how we're going to get you out of this mess.'

An idea occurred to her, as she tipped the bottle up so that the last few drops ran down into the teat.

Lucky, she thought. I'm going to call you Lucky. Maybe the name will bring us luck, because, oh boy, we're certainly going to need it.

7

A DARING PLAN

It felt so good to be holding Lucky in her arms that Afra could hardly bear to part with him.

'It's not for long,' she whispered. 'You have to go back in your box now, Lucky.'

Someone had left a newspaper in the pouch in front of her seat. She took it out and laid it in the bottom of the box. Then awkwardly, she disengaged his long arms, which had wrapped themselves round her own, and planted him back into his box. He seemed inclined to climb out again.

'No!' she said, knowing he wouldn't understand.

She remembered suddenly how Bella, her friend Tom's little sister, liked to carry a soft toy with her everywhere she went. Maybe Lucky would settle if he had something to cuddle too.

She felt in the bag by her feet and pulled out a scarf. It was a pretty one, which Minette had given her, but she screwed it into a ball and tucked it down by Lucky's face. He grasped it immediately, and began to nibble at it with his lips, and rub it over his face. Quickly, she replaced the towel and secured it again with the strips from Mwape's old shirt.

She was only just in time. She had almost forgotten the passengers in the front of the plane, who seemed somehow miles away beyond the empty seats, and she was shocked when one of the women turned round.

'You doing OK back there, kids? How are the bananas coming along?' she called out.

Afra smiled, but her heart was hammering.

'Just fine,' she called back. 'Us and the bananas both.'

The woman laughed and turned round again.

Afra looked sideways at Mwape, grateful that he hadn't joined in this conversation with flourishes of his own. She was surprised to see that his face was alive with excitement.

'I know what we can do,' he said in a conspiratorial voice, beaming at her.

'Oh? What?' She sounded guarded.

'Listen, this is a very good plan. It is exciting too. Like an adventure.'

Her heart sank. Mwape's exuberance was unnerving.

He saw her doubtful look and smiled encouragingly.

'No, no, you do not believe me, but you will. I have remembered something.'

'Remembered what?'

'Sokomuntu!'

'Sokomuntu? What's that?'

'It is a place in Zambia. A kind of refuge for chimpanzees. They have so many animals there.'

'What sort of refuge?' said Afra suspiciously. 'Is it like a zoo? Are they all caged up?'

'No! I went there when I was a kid, with my school. There are big fences, very high, so that the chimpanzees cannot get out, but inside there are trees and grass, and they can do whatever they like. They play, you know, like chasing each other, and wrestling, and jumping around in the branches.'

Afra's grip tightened on the box. It sounded too good to be true, a perfect solution for Lucky, but already she was feeling a pang of loss.

He won't be mine if he goes there, she thought, and I guess he is now, sort of.

She gave her head a little shake, trying to clear it. She had to think about what was best for Lucky. She mustn't let her feelings get in the way. 'Where is this place?' she asked. 'How would we get him there?'

Mwape leaned towards her across the aisle, looking down the plane to check that no one else could hear.

'It is in Zambia,' he whispered, watching her face.

She frowned at him.

'But you can't take chimps across the border,' she said. 'Daniel said so.'

'I know!' he chuckled, and slapped his knee with his hand. 'That is why we will have a big adventure.'

She stared at him.

'Mwape, we're not James Bond and Jackie Chan. We're not even Arnold Schwarzenegger. We're not doing this for fun. We have a baby chimp here who has to get to safety.'

'Of course. I know that.' He was not at all crestfallen by her discouragement. 'The plan is a good one. I have been thinking about it carefully.'

He was speaking more earnestly now, and was building shapes in the air with his hands as he spoke.

'We cannot leave him here in Congo. He will be taken to a zoo. I know the zoos here. They are very bad. Very crowded and small, and the animals' food is not enough for them. So there is only one logical alternative. We have to get him out of the country.'

'Yes. OK. But the border guards—'

'We will not meet any border guards. They are only on the roads. We will cross the border in another place, far from these kinds of official people.'

'Where? How?'

'Lubumbashi is very near to the border with Zambia. Only a few kilometres. And Sokomuntu is not far from the border on the other side. We will go on foot.'

'On foot?' She stared at him. 'But people are sure to see us and ask questions, especially if we're miles from a road. You know what country people are like. They always want to know everything.'

Mwape waved his hands airily.

'They will not see us! We will go very carefully, after dark even.'

'After dark?' said Afra, in a small voice. 'Through the forest?'

She didn't want to admit it to Mwape, but she was scared of being in the open at night. In Kenya she had run out once into the middle of the night, and had made her way across deserted countryside. Hyenas had prowled close by, and lions and leopards had not been far away. She had nearly died of terror.

Mwape seemed to read her thoughts.

'It is not forest like Congo,' he said. 'Just some small acacia trees. You can walk easily when there is a moon, and there are no dangerous wild animals now in northern Zambia.'

As he spoke, a slight unease crossed his face.

He's not sure, Afra thought. He's just saying it.

'But how are we going to carry Lucky?' New objections were crowding into her mind.

'Lucky?' He looked puzzled.

'Oh sorry. That's what I decided to call the chimp. I reckoned he'd need whole mountains of luck to get through.'

Mwape nodded.

'Lucky. It is a nice name.' He seemed to have forgotten her question, but came back to it a moment later. 'We will not be able to carry him in the box. It is too difficult and cumbersome. It would be better just to take him like a child. To carry him ourselves.'

Afra saw a mental picture of herself walking through an acacia woodland with a baby chimp in her arms. It seemed impossible and unreal. She wasn't used to the sensation that Mwape's plans were stirring up in her. In the past, she had always been the one to think up daring schemes, to race ahead of her friends, Tom and Joseph, silencing their objections and carrying them along by the strength of her will-power. But Mwape's exuberant sense of adventure alarmed her. She needed time to think things out, to make sensible plans. She was responsible now for the creature in her lap. The rest of his life depended on the decisions she would make.

To give herself time, she looked sideways out of the window. There was no longer a dense carpet of green below. The forest was patchy, broken up with fields and stretches of dry brown earth, where the trees had long since been felled. They were moving out of chimp territory, into a very different kind of land.

'Are you sure about Sokomuntu?' she said, turning back to Mwape.

74

'Sure? I am certain. It is heaven for a chimpanzee. OK, it is not heaven, like his own piece of forest, but a second-best heaven. A safe place. With others like him. This is the best thing we can do, Afra. You must believe me.'

He sat back in his seat and a satisfied smile settled on his lips.

'But what about your dad? He'll expect you to go home, won't he? You can't just take off into the blue. And Minette, the person I'm supposed to be meeting, she'll totally freak out if I suddenly disappear. And Mrs Hamble. She's sure to stick to me like glue.'

He looked at her almost pityingly.

'We will telephone from the airport at Lubumbashi. I will tell my father that I am visiting a friend. You will telephone your person and tell them something. And for Mrs Hamble, I don't know! You must think of a good story.'

She saw herself momentarily through his eyes, a tiresome girl, thinking up objections to his lovely plan, too scared to grasp the brilliant solution he had devised to Lucky's problem. She bit her lip. He wasn't going to despise her. She was capable of anything, taking any risk, facing any danger, to save Lucky.

'OK,' she said, trying to sound brisk and decisive. 'We'll do it.'

She was about to say more when the co-pilot's voice floated through the cabin.

'Ladies and gentlemen, please fasten your seat belts and put your seats in an upright position. We are about to land at Lubumbashi.'

8

MIXED MESSAGES

Afra's heart was in her mouth as the plane landed bumpily on the tarmac and came to a shuddering halt. There was no sound from inside the box, and she guessed that the second bottle of milk had sent Lucky off to sleep.

'Just stay that way, baby,' she whispered. 'This is not going to be easy.'

The sun was already plunging down towards the horizon, bathing the land all around in brilliant light. Afra stepped out of the plane last, shielding herself behind Mwape, who was walking jauntily ahead of her on the balls of his feet, as if he was enjoying every moment.

They walked into the airport building. It was big but almost deserted. Dusk would soon be falling and no more flights were expected that day.

Mrs Hamble was already sitting slumped on a chair just inside the door. She was talking to the pilot who was leaning down to catch her words. She caught sight of Afra and smiled blearily at her.

'There you are, dear. We're just discussing what to do with you.'

Surreptitiously, Afra put Lucky's box down in a corner behind a row of chairs and went up to her.

'I'll be fine,' she said, trying to sound breezy. 'Don't worry about me.'

She wanted to tell Mrs Hamble that she had an old friend in Lubumbashi, who would be coming out to pick her up, or that she and Mwape had discovered they were long-lost cousins and she would be going to stay with his family, but neither story would sound at all convincing. She had no idea how she was going to get Mrs Hamble out of the way.

'Peter Mpundi's going to get the people here to radio Luangwa and get a message to your daddy's friend,' Mrs Hamble was saying with a ghastly smile. 'You'll be quite safe, till we get you to her. I'll make sure of that.'

Afra squirmed. She was aware that Mwape was coming up behind her and was afraid he would join in, suggest something with too much misguided enthusiasm, and make Mrs Hamble suspicious. She felt an urgent need to get away from them both.

'Are you going to radio Luangwa now?' she said to Peter Mpundi. 'Can I come with you?'

He smiled down at her, looking indulgent and avuncular.

Any minute now he's going to pat me on the head, thought Afra, and her own smile set in her cheeks like cooling lava.

But Peter Mpundi seemed to sense her withdrawal.

'Come with me, then,' he said, and he began to walk towards the back of the arrivals hall.

Afra cast an agonized backwards glance at Mwape, caught his eye and nodded significantly towards the box. To her relief he merely nodded back in acknowledgement, and sat down on the nearest chair to it, as if he was keeping guard.

The radio operator knew Peter Mpundi. They spoke to each other in French, and Afra couldn't follow their rapid conversation, but she watched anxiously as the operator put through the call. She was feeling numb. Decisions were being taken out of her hands. She was caught on a nightmarish conveyor belt that was carrying her away from her own independence, and from her chance to rescue Lucky.

'Peter!'

A loud cheerful voice behind her made her turn her head. A big man was bearing down on Peter Mpundi from behind. Peter broke away from the operator's desk and walked over to talk to him. Afra felt a tingle of hope. Her numbness receded.

The operator finished his call and looked up at her.

'Do not worry,' he said. 'I have spoken to the

people at Luangwa. They know that you are here. Your friend is expecting you to fly to meet her there tomorrow morning.'

Afra could hear Peter Mpundi approach from behind. She flashed a smile at the operator.

'That's great,' she said. 'Thank you.'

She moved quickly away from him towards Peter. He seemed about to push past her to speak to the operator, and her heart lurched, but then a crackle came from the radio, and the operator began to speak into it. Peter waved goodbye to the operator and walked away from him beside Afra.

'It's so good,' she said. 'They sent my dad's friend a message from Mumbasa. She's coming from Luangwa to fetch me now.'

'Now?' He frowned. 'How?'

'Someone's bringing her in a plane. I don't know. That's what the guy told me. She says I just have to wait here. They'll be along in half an hour. The plane took off an hour ago.'

'But the airport is closing now. It will be dark soon.'

'They said they'd make it in time. It's still only half-past five.'

Her fists were balled so tightly that her finger-nails were biting into the palms of her hands. He shook his head and seemed about to say more, but they had reached Mrs Hamble again.

'It's all arranged, Mrs Hamble,' Afra said with

breathy enthusiasm. She glanced quickly towards the box, but Mwape was still sitting on the chair in front of it, obscuring it from her view. 'Minette's on her way here now. I have to wait for her. She said so.'

Mrs Hamble looked up with a wan smile of relief.

'So all's well that ends well. My, what a day you've had, you poor mite. We'll wait in the cafe, shall we? They'll give us a cup of tea there.'

'Oh, *you* don't need to wait with me. You still don't look very well, Mrs Hamble. You ought to be lying down.' Afra felt ashamed of her gushing concern, but she pressed on. 'You look real pale and sickly. I'll be fine here.'

'No no.' Mrs Hamble winced as she shook her head. 'You're my responsibility. I'd never forgive myself if anything—'

'But I am here,' said Mwape suddenly, standing up and coming across to join them. 'I am waiting for my father. He is coming to collect me. We will stay here with Afra until her friend comes, then we can take them both to a good hotel for the night.'

He looked serious and sensible, his excited manner gone. Afra held her breath.

'Well . . .' Mrs Hamble began.

'They're waiting for us!' fluted one of the American women, flapping a hand towards Mrs Hamble from the doorway, through which Afra could see that a minibus had pulled up. 'Are you folks coming? We have our lift into town here.'

'Don't worry,' said Peter Mpundi, reaching a hand down and hooking it under Mrs Hamble's elbow to help her to her feet. 'You go and lie down now. You are not well. I will keep my eye on these two kids.'

'You will?' She turned to him gratefully. 'You're not leaving the airport yet?'

'Not yet. I have to file my report. Come. The minibus is waiting.'

Mrs Hamble put out her hands and rested them on Afra's shoulders. There was real affection in her eyes. Afra felt a pang of guilt.

'You're a good girl,' Mrs Hamble said. 'What a shame your holiday got off to such a bad . . .' She staggered suddenly, and put a hand up to her head.

'You look terribly sick, Mrs Hamble,' said Afra, and this time her concern was genuine. 'Thank you for looking after me. It was very kind of you. I just hope your headache's better soon.'

Mrs Hamble couldn't answer. She reached out and squeezed Afra's hand, then let Peter Mpundi lead her out to the waiting minibus.

As soon as they were out of earshot, Afra turned to Mwape.

'I didn't know your dad was coming to collect you.'

'He isn't.' Mwape was looking pleased with himself. 'I just told her to make her go away.'

'Then what do we do next?' she whispered. 'How are we going to get out of here?'

He was already starting away from her towards a desk marked Information.

'Wait,' he said. 'First I have to call my father.'

There was a new edginess in his voice, and as he walked away she saw that his bounciness had gone. She had moved round to look behind the chairs to check on Lucky's box, when she saw that Peter Mpundi was standing on the far side of the hall, pointing her out to a man in uniform. She gave them a little wave and sank down on one of the chairs. Mwape was talking on a phone that someone had placed on the Information counter for him. He looked tense. He was tapping the side of his leg with the flat of his left hand.

He put the receiver down and came towards her. He looked dejected, but as he neared her, and saw that her eyes were on him, he shook his shoulders, as if trying to throw something off, and made an effort to resume his cheery manner.

'Did you speak to him? Your father, I mean?' Afra asked eagerly. 'Is it OK?'

'My father? No!' He was trying to sound careless, but his bitterness showed through. 'It was that woman, my stepmother.'

'Your stepmother? Is your real mother – I mean, is she still alive?'

'Yes, of course. My father divorced her. I wanted to speak to him, but my stepmother would not allow me. She never likes me.'

'Oh.'

'She is so selfish. She is always angry. I hate her.'

He sounded younger than his fourteen years and Afra was afraid that his will-power was ebbing away.

'Did you send him a message?' she said urgently. 'You are still coming with me, aren't you?' There was no time now to be distracted by Mwape's family life.

'Oh yes. I told her, "You can tell my father," I told her, "I have gone to visit my mother. My real mother. I will return when I like." I am sorry I could not speak to him. When she is not there, my father is sometimes very helpful to me. Perhaps he would have helped us. Perhaps he would have known what to do.'

'What?' Afra's blood ran cold. 'You mean you would have told your dad about Lucky?'

Mwape shrugged.

'Yes. My father is very clever, and he knows wildlife. He would like maybe to keep Lucky for himself.'

'But Sokomuntu! The chimp reserve! Lucky can't end up as a pet. You know he can't! We *talked* about this. You *agreed*. A heaven for

84

chimps, you said. We're going to take Lucky there, through the forest!'

Her anger shook him out of himself. He seemed to snap back into focus.

'You are right,' he said, with unaccustomed humility. 'I forgot for a moment. I was thinking about my father, how to please him. But he was there, in the room! I heard him! With her! He didn't even want to speak with me. So we will go off to Zambia, and then I will visit my mother. I can do it easily. She lives in Chingola. It is very close to Sokomuntu. And my father will worry about me. Why should I care?'

'I know how you feel about your dad,' said Afra, a mixture of sympathy and exasperation in her voice. 'As it happens, I really do. But we have to get going, Mwape. We're in danger here. Lucky's going to wake up any moment and then we'll be in real trouble.'

'It's OK. I know.' He smiled at her, and she saw to her relief that both his dejection and his exaggerated bounciness seemed to have gone. He looked serious and confident, almost grown-up.

'It's going to be easy,' he said. 'You just pick up the box and we'll walk slowly out of those doors. I'll take your bag. If anyone asks where we're going, we will say we want to wait outside because it is cooler there. OK?'

'OK.'

She was leaning on his confidence with relief.

She stood up and took a quick look round the hall. Peter Mpundi had disappeared. No one else was looking in their direction. She looked behind the chair.

The box was still there, but the towel that covered it had been pulled off. The box was empty. Lucky had gone.

9

THE PICK-UP VAN

Afra went cold with fright.

He's been stolen, she thought. Someone stole him!

A rush of anger hit her, almost blinding her. Then she heard Mwape say, 'He has run away. Outside, maybe. He is trying to find his forest.'

She looked wildly round the hall. Mwape was right. No one had come to this corner. No one could have found the box and lifted Lucky out of it without being seen. No one even knew there was a baby chimp in the airport at all. Lucky must have climbed out of the box himself.

He's sick and weak, she thought. He could hardly crawl out of his box on the plane. He can't be far away.

Her brain was working more clearly now. She bent down and looked under the row of chairs. He wasn't there. She started towards a nearby counter, from which the staff had long since gone away, but then a movement caught her eye. Her scarf, the one she had tucked down into the box beside Lucky, was moving along the ground as if of its own accord. She looked sideways, and saw that it was being pulled behind a litter bin.

She darted over to it, and pulled the bin out from the wall. The little chimp was huddled behind it, rocking backwards and forwards, looking up at her with round, frightened eyes.

'Lucky!' she breathed. 'Oh, thank God. I found you!'

A plaintive sound, half-whimper, half-squeak, came from Lucky's throat. Still tightly clutching one end of Afra's scarf, he uncoiled himself, took two steps towards her on his hind legs and held up his arms like a child, wanting to be carried.

She leaned down and scooped him up in her arms.

'Afra! Hurry! I think they have seen us. We have to get out of here!'

Mwape was behind her. He was holding her bag and his own was slung over his shoulder. Afra looked round. Peter Mpundi was talking to the radio operator, who had emerged from behind his desk, and was gesticulating towards them angrily.

Throwing caution to the wind, Afra bolted towards the big glass doors leading to the airport forecourt. She heard shouts echoing round the arrivals hall behind her, and Peter Mpundi's angry voice calling out, 'Stop, you kids. What kind of a game are you playing?'

Then she was outside in the grey twilight with Mwape racing along beside her.

She looked frantically up and down the long concrete strip that fronted the airport building. There was nowhere to hide. Everywhere was open, and exposed to view.

'Quick! Follow me!' said Mwape, who was already bolting across the road to a car park.

Afra darted after him. She had been clutching Lucky to her chest, both of his long arms were wrapped securely round her neck, and his legs tightly encircled her waist. He was used to clinging onto his mother as she swung through the forest canopy. He was in no danger of falling.

They reached the car park, took shelter behind a minibus, and looked back. The radio operator and Peter Mpundi had run out of the building behind them and were talking excitedly to three uniformed guards, who had been sitting outside the entrance.

'Lower your head!' hissed Mwape, ducking behind the minibus. 'They are pointing at us.'

'What are we going to do?' Afra was almost squeaking with fright. 'They'll catch us. They'll take Lucky away. We'll be in terrible trouble.'

'No.' Mwape's voice was hoarse with excitement. 'They will not find us. We will be too clever for them.'

His eyes were darting about the car park. Unconsciously, his hands were stretched out straight as if he was preparing to make karate chops.

He thinks he's Jackie Chan, thought Afra. Why did I get him mixed up in all this? He's a crazy, crazy guy.

Mwape grunted with triumph.

'Look over there,' he whispered. 'That pick-up. There's a cover on the back. We can hide underneath it.'

He had already snatched up the bags and was sidling, cat-like, around the side of the minibus.

'Follow me. Quickly!' he breathed. 'Look, they are coming this way.'

Afra's arms tightened round Lucky again. His hairy head was tucked under her chin and his warm smell was in her nostrils.

If they try to get him away from me, I'll fight them. I'll do anything. I'll just kill them, she thought, and the idea gave her courage. A moment later, she had climbed up into the pick-up beside Mwape and the tarpaulin was covering them both.

It was almost dark now, and pitch-black in the back of the pick-up. She could hear Mwape fumbling around on the floor.

'Quiet!' she hissed. 'They'll hear you!'

He grunted in reply, then pulled at her arm. She felt a piece of old sacking between her fingers and gasped as Mwape pulled it over her head. Then she understood. She sat back against the side of the truck and tried to pull the sacking over her. It was too small. She thought quickly, wrapped a corner round her fingers so that they wouldn't show and whispered into Mwape's ear.

'It won't cover us both. Take the other corner. We'll have to hold it up like a screen.'

Mwape grabbed the corner from her and she felt the sacking tighten as he held it up. She wriggled close to him, trying to make sure that no bit of her was showing.

Voices could be heard clearly now. They were taut with fury. Peter Mpundi, the radio operator and several others whose voices she did not recognize were rapidly approaching.

'You go down that way,' Peter Mpundi was calling out. 'They might be trying to run to the main gate. We'll search the car park. They won't get out of the airport. Security's too tight.'

There was a sudden silence. Afra felt Lucky move in her arms. His hair was tickling her nose.

I mustn't sneeze. I must not sneeze, she told herself.

She moved her arm a little, and Lucky settled down again. His warm body lay tightly against hers, his arms tense.

He knows I'm scared, Afra thought. He feels it too.

A hand slapped suddenly against the outside of the pick-up, making her jump with fright. She could sense that Lucky was drawing in his breath, ready to whimper, or to scream with fear, and she forced herself to relax her muscles, trying to reassure him.

'Look under this thing,' Peter Mpundi's voice said.

He was no more than a few centimetres away, on the other side of the tarpaulin. She heard the stiff canvas creak as it was pulled back, and she shut her eyes, squeezing them tight, hardly daring to breathe, willing her arm not to tremble as she tried to hold the sacking screen perfectly still.

Quiet, Lucky. Just keep quiet, she was shouting in her head. Don't move. Stay still.

After what seemed like an age, the corner of the tarpaulin clattered back into place again.

'If they're not in there, then where *are* they?' Peter Mpundi sounded worried now, as well as angry.

'Perhaps they went back into the airport building, sir,' a new voice said. 'Why don't we go back and look there?'

One of the guards, thought Afra.

The footsteps were receding now, and the voices growing fainter. Then, just nearby, a car door slammed and an engine spluttered into life. A moment later, a gleam of headlights, slipping through a chink in the tarpaulin, penetrated the sacking. Then the car sped away, and it was totally dark again.

Afra was about to drop the sacking and scramble out of the pick-up when another sound made her freeze again. Someone was unlocking the door to the pick-up's driver's seat. Someone was climbing into it.

'David!' a man's voice called out in Swahili. 'I can take you and the others with me. Get in the back. I'll give you a lift into town.'

Afra had begun to feel a flicker of confidence, a little surge of triumph, but fear seized her again. Her bones turned to water. Her skin was prickling all over. She could hear more feet now, running towards the pick-up.

This is it, she thought. In one minute, half a minute even, they'll find us.

She braced herself for discovery, as if warding off a blow, then, with incredulous joy, heard the driver say, 'Are there only two of you? No need to go in the back. Come in the front with me.'

A moment later, both the two front doors slammed, the engine started and the pick-up began to bump along the potholed surface of the car park.

She felt Mwape's hand grasp her arm.

'Watch out,' he whispered. 'They might check the back at the gate.'

The fine dust in the sacking was really irritating her eyes and nose now, and she was desperate to sneeze. She wrinkled her nose, trying to stop herself.

As if he had caught the impulse from her, Lucky suddenly sneezed. The sound was so familiar and human it almost made her snort with laughter. There was no danger that the men in front had heard him. The car was making too much noise.

The pick-up had gathered speed. It was on a smoother surface now, on what felt like tarmac. It slowed down, and Afra felt a jolt as it stopped altogether.

'OK. Goodnight!' she heard the driver call, then the pick-up speeded up again.

They were past the security gate, out of the airport, and on the open road, on their way into Lubumbashi town.

10

ALONE IN THE DARK

Afra's mind raced ahead as the pick-up bumped along the road into town. They had managed to escape from the airport, but in the most disastrously spectacular way. Everyone would be after them now. Peter Mpundi was sure to raise a real hue and cry. Within an hour or two, every policeman, every shopkeeper, every barman in Lubumbashi, would know that a boy and girl were on the run.

Had Lucky been seen? She couldn't be sure. If he had, things were worse still. As it was, their chances of getting out of Lubumbashi and finding their way to the Zambian border were horribly slim.

The pick-up braked suddenly, and Afra almost toppled over. Mwape was peering out through a chink in the tarpaulin, and she almost pulled him back, afraid he would be seen. Then she heard one of the doors of the front cab open.

'Good night! Thanks for the lift,' a man's voice said.

The door shut, and the pick-up began to move

off, but then the man shouted something and the driver jerked to a stop again.

Afra couldn't pick up the driver's answer, but the pick-up began to move again, and turned sharply left, tilting sideways and bumping over rough ground as if the driver had steered it off the road. Then the engine was switched off and the driver's door opened.

'What about the car? Is it safe here?' she heard the driver say, and her heart sank as a third voice replied, 'Don't worry. I'll stay here and wait for you.'

It lifted again as the first man said, 'No, why? It's OK here. Come in and have a beer.'

The pick-up shook a little as the third man clambered out from the middle seat, the doors slammed shut and the key clicked in the lock. Then the men's footsteps receded.

Afra was already scrambling to the back end of the pick-up.

'Quick! Now! This our chance,' she hissed to Mwape, who was still sitting, immobile, peering out through the crack.

'I don't know this place,' he said complainingly. 'It is far out of town. I thought they would take us further in.'

'Yes, where there would be lights and people and police everywhere,' Afra said impatiently. 'We're not exactly inconspicuous. You don't exactly melt into a crowd if you're carrying a baby chimpanzee.'

Mwape didn't answer. He crawled past her and lifted back the tarpaulin.

'Do you think I don't know all that?' he said, sounding offended. 'I just thought it would be better if we could be near to a shop. We have to buy food, and get water for Lucky's bottle.'

Humbled, Afra scrambled out of the pick-up after him, with Lucky clinging like a limpet to her chest.

You need this guy, she told herself sternly. You can't do this alone. Don't keep putting him down.

She looked around. They were on a long straight road that ran ahead, a faint pale streak, into the darkness. Clumps of high grass and a few trees seemed to border it. Several unshaded lights shone out from a row of houses set back a little way on one side of the road.

Mwape was looking both ways, as if trying to assess where they were.

'I do recognize this place,' he said at last. 'It's not too far from town, I think, after all. Maybe two or three kilometres. You'll have to wait here, out of sight. I'll go and get some food.'

'But they'll be looking out for you.' Afra felt a surge of panic at the idea of being left alone, in the dark, in this unfamiliar place.

'They won't look for one boy, on his own,' Mwape said, and she could hear excitement tinge

97

his voice again. 'Anyway, my house is on the other side of town. No one knows me here.'

Afra swallowed.

'All right,' she said. 'Where am I going to wait?'

'Not here. It is too near the houses. We will walk a little way into Lubumbashi. We will find a good place.'

They moved off down the road. To her surprise, Afra saw that Mwape was still carrying her bag, and his own was slung over his shoulder. She felt a little less vulnerable.

They walked along in silence. Afra could feel the heat of the day, imprisoned in the road surface, rising off it. She shifted Lucky in her arms. He was surprisingly heavy for a small animal. He felt solid, as if his little body was made up of dense bone and muscle. In response, Lucky clambered up her arm and hauled himself onto her shoulders, then he sat like a child, his hands clasped round her forehead, his legs dangling down on each side of her neck.

She felt a new exultation. The little chimp was becoming more confident with her, more at ease. There was a bond between them now. She could feel it in her bones. It was as strong as a piece of elastic, tying them together.

Mwape suddenly stopped and grabbed her arm.

'A car!' he said. 'Quick!'

A moment later he had pulled her off the road into the partial obscurity of the trees.

Car lights were approaching fast. Afra wanted to run further back, away from the road, but Mwape said urgently, 'Stay still. It is easier for them to see something that moves.'

The car was almost level with them now. Afra felt the light from the headlamps sweep over her, as cruelly shocking as a douse of cold water. She shut her eyes, willing herself not to move. Then it had gone, and she opened them again and let out her breath. Red tail lights were disappearing rapidly down the road.

'It was the pilot. Peter Mpundi. Did you see him?' Mwape said exultantly, slapping his hands together. 'He failed to catch us again!'

Afra sat down suddenly on the hard dry earth. Her legs had simply given way under her. She wanted to cry. She had wished for nothing more than to escape from Peter Mpundi and everyone else who would soon be hunting for her, but the sight of those red lights moving inexorably away, the strangeness of this open place, and the dark hours of the night stretching ahead filled her with desolation.

'I'm so hungry,' she said, gulping back tears.

'You must stay here.' Mwape was still on his feet, and his voice floated down to her out of the dark. 'I will go and find food. I will come back very soon.'

'How will you find me?'

He laughed confidently.

'I am a magician! I can see in the dark!'

He began to walk away. She resisted the impulse to reach out for his hand and beg him to stay.

'No, but really, Mwape,' she said. 'How will you find me again?'

'See there?' He pointed to the tree nearest the roadside. Its topmost branch was bare and dead, and stood out against the star-studded sky like a huge crooked elbow on a black sequinned coat. 'I will look for that. I will find you.'

A moment later he had gone. Afra heard a rustle as he walked through a clump of brittle grass, then a few footfalls on the road, then nothing more.

She wanted to call out, 'Please, Mwape. Don't just go off and leave me. Promise you'll come back,' but she managed not to.

She sat listening to the night that wrapped itself around her, close and dark. There were crickets rasping all around, and somewhere not far away the call of a nightjar.

We're all alone, she thought, me and a chimpanzee. And everyone here is after us. Prof doesn't know where I am, and Minette doesn't either, and they're all going to be so mad at me. Anyway, I probably broke about 150 laws today, and I'll end up in jail, and they'll cart Lucky off to a zoo, and no one will ever find me, or visit me, or anything.

Lucky had slipped down off her shoulders and was sitting in her lap. He had been grasping her T-shirt with one hard little hand, but it gradually relaxed, and she knew he was asleep.

'Goodnight, honey,' she whispered. 'Don't worry. It's worth it. I'd do it over again. I'm going to get you someplace you can be happy if it's the last thing I do.'

She tried to imagine the journey ahead, but saw only a frightening blank.

I don't have any idea where I am, or what kind of countryside this is, or if there are people around here, or which direction Zambia is even, she thought helplessly. I just have to trust Mwape, and I only met him today. I don't understand him. He keeps changing all the time. One minute he's being James Bond, then he's just a little boy who wants to please his daddy, then he's sort of OK, and really sensible and everything. I wish he was Joseph. Or Tom. I know them. I could trust *them*.

Her legs were stiffening up and a twig was digging uncomfortably into her thigh. She moved gingerly, not wanting to alarm Lucky, but he merely grunted, sighed, and settled himself again against her chest.

The minutes ticked by. Her eyes were now quite used to the dark. A quarter moon had risen. It cast a faint, spectral light, barely enough to see past the trunks of the nearest trees. She had no idea if she was sitting on the edge of a great forest, or if she was in a small clump of trees between farmers' fields.

Then suddenly, she heard a new sound, a patter of paws and a rustle of dry leaves. An animal was approaching. Unconsciously, Afra's arms tightened around Lucky. Her heart thumped violently once, then settled into a fast fearful rhythm. Mwape had said there were no leopards or hyenas here, but how did he know?

She was about to panic, to scramble to her feet and run blindly away, when she heard a puzzled woof.

'It's only a dog!' she breathed, and she wanted to break out into a wild guffaw of relief.

The dog had scented her. He was growling, approaching her cautiously, circling round her, the smell of the chimpanzee puzzling and alarming him.

He'll bark if I'm not careful. If there's a dog here there must be people around. He'll give me away, thought Afra.

She sat still and forced herself to be calm.

'Good dog,' she said quietly, putting all the reassurance she could into her voice. 'It's OK. It's just me and Lucky. No need to go crazy now. Good dog.'

The dog lifted its head and barked once, but without conviction. It stood uncertainly for a while, and she could see the glow of its eyes. Then it scratched for a moment at the ground, as if trying to impress her, emitted a little whine, and lay down a few metres away.

'No,' Afra said firmly. 'You can't stay here. You'll bark when Mwape comes. Go away. Go home.'

The dog heard the sharpness in her voice. It stood up and whined again.

'Go home!' Afra commanded again, as loudly as she dared. To her relief, the dog turned and trotted away.

It seemed as if hours had passed when at last she heard footsteps on the road. She had passed into an almost trance-like state, half-sleeping, half-dreaming, but she was alert at once.

The footsteps slowed, and she heard a tentative cough. She sat motionless. Why hadn't she and Mwape agreed on a signal? How did she know if it was Mwape out there? They might have caught him, and forced him to tell them where she was hiding. It could be a policeman standing out there, coughing in the road, or Peter Mpundi, or just a man walking home from his work in the town.

'Afra, it's me. Mwape. Are you there?'

Her heart leaped with relief. There was no mistaking the sound of his voice. It was Mwape all right. He had come back. He hadn't abandoned her. She felt weak with relief and gratitude.

'Here! I'm here!' She rose carefully to her feet, trying not to disturb Lucky. 'Did you get anything? Any food, I mean? Was it OK?'

He was coming towards her through the trees.

'Yes. I have some food and water. But we have to go now, quickly.' He sounded scared, and his usual bravado was gone.

'Why? What happened?'

'They're setting up roadblocks, stopping cars, asking everyone if they've seen two runaway kids. I nearly ran into a bunch of policemen back there. I had to go round away from the road. And we're right near houses here. I passed them just now, on this side of the road. Come on, Afra. We can't stay here. We have to get away as far as we can. Tonight.'

11

THE TRACK TO THE SOUTH

Afra began to run. She didn't know where she was going, and she could see no more than a little way ahead, but Mwape had frightened her and she was desperate to get away from the road. Lucky woke up at once and began to chatter with fear, flinging his long hairy arms around her neck and clinging on like a little black rider to its horse.

She had gone no more than a hundred metres when Mwape caught up with her.

'What are you doing? Are you crazy? Do you want us to be lost?'

She stopped, confused.

'I – I'm sorry. I didn't think. I just wanted to get away.'

'Well, you have to think. We can't leave the road. We need it. We must find a track running off it to take us to the south. How else will we find our way? There are little farms everywhere here. You can't just run across the countryside.' His voice was raw with fright.

'I'm sorry,' Afra said again. She felt humiliated. Mwape was right, of course. He knew

Lubumbashi. He lived here. She had no choice but to follow his lead.

He was already walking back to the road.

If I'd gone just a bit further we really would have been lost, she thought. I was so dumb.

Dry pods and twigs from the acacia trees crackled underfoot, sounding loud in her ears. What if the dog heard them and came back? He'd be sure to bark at them, then people might come and investigate.

Mwape had dropped Afra's bag and the two plastic carriers of food in the place where she'd been sitting. It was lucky that the bags were white, and gleamed dully in the thin moonlight, or they might not have found them again.

Afra picked up one of the bags, and Mwape took the other in his spare hand. Cautiously, they set off once more along the road, ready to dive off it again if another car came past, but as five minutes past, then ten, then twenty, with no sign of any more traffic, Afra began to relax.

'No one will pass us,' Mwape said confidently, as if reading her thoughts. 'It is late now. People do not like to go around at night.'

'Except crazies like us,' said Afra, trying to make amends.

Mwape laughed.

'You are a crazy person,' he said. 'I am simply a genius.'

Afra had been worried only about passing cars,

and she didn't see the man walking quietly along the road towards them until it was too late to turn aside. He was moving fast and silently, his eyes down, looking at the road. Mwape gave Afra a gentle push and she took the hint and walked off to the side, while Mwape walked directly into the stranger's path, swaggering a little to show his confidence.

'Good evening, brother,' he said in a friendly voice, when the man was almost abreast of him.

The man started with surprise and recoiled, as if from a threat.

'Yes, good evening,' he said nervously, and without a second glance at Mwape, walked on. Afra had moved back to Mwape's side, when the man called back to them, 'Brother, be careful. There are some militia men further on, just before you come to the gas station. They have been drinking too much beer.'

Mwape turned back to him.

'Thank you, but we are nearly at my sister's home. It is just beside the track that goes south, towards the border. Do you know where it is? I am afraid I will not see it in the dark, and my wife is tired already. I don't want to walk further than is necessary.'

Afra listened with stunned admiration, resisting the temptation to giggle. Mwape had assumed the voice of a grown-up man, and he sounded easy and confident.

'It's not far,' the man said. 'You will see a big tree, an old one, beside the road, and there is a thorn fence with a gate in it. The track goes off there. But be careful, like I told you. It's not only the militia. There are thieves on this road at night sometimes.'

Afra saw a faint movement in the darkness as he waved a hand at them, and then he had gone.

'That was brilliant, Mwape,' she said quietly, as they walked on, 'finding out where the track starts from, I mean, and making him think we were grown-up. They're looking for kids, not an adult couple, so he'd never have suspected us. He didn't seem to see Lucky, either.'

She could sense that Mwape was preening himself.

'He did see Lucky,' he said. 'He thought he was a child. He looks like a child, in the dark.'

'Oh wow!' Afra really did giggle this time. 'I've gotten myself a husband and a kid all in five minutes. Must be a world record.'

Her spirits had inexplicably lifted again. They had surmounted another danger. Mwape had cleverly found out where to go. And they had food.

The thought of food reminded her that she was hungry.

'What did you buy?' she said. 'This bag's so heavy it's biting into my fingers.'

'There wasn't much in the shop. I got what I

could. Three bottles of water, bread, biscuits, a tin of sardines. Some bananas. I wanted to get eggs but they didn't have any. We will have to be a little hungry, maybe.'

'Good thing you didn't. How would we cook them?'

'We could make a fire.' Suddenly he had switched to being an enthusiastic fantasist again. 'In the old way, without matches.'

'Do you know how to cook eggs without a pan too?'

She realized she was being too sarcastic and bit her lip. But Mwape wasn't listening to her.

'Look there, that big tree,' he said. 'That must be it.'

He broke into a run, eager to make sure, and called softly back to her, 'Yes, this is it. The thorn fence is here.'

She was looking beyond him, her eyes widening with fright. A big truck had suddenly appeared round a bend in the road, and it was careering towards them at full speed. She raced after Mwape, who was already disappearing off the road into the track, and they huddled together by the thorn fence as the truck roared past. Above the noise of the engine they could hear throaty shouts and men's voices singing.

'The militia,' Mwape murmured in Afra's ear. 'They are very drunk. Look, they are going on.

They didn't see us. Thank God! They are very cruel men. Very violent. If they catch us . . .'

He shuddered.

The sound of the truck faded away. Afra put the bag of food down on the ground, and shifted Lucky, who felt like a dead weight on her shoulders.

'Mwape, it's no good. I'm worn out. I have to stop and eat something and rest soon. Lucky's so heavy, and I've hardly eaten a thing all day.'

She stopped, afraid she was about to cry.

Mwape was peering down the track ahead.

'I know this place!' he said. 'I came here once with my father to visit an old sick man. It is so nice down there. Just a little way on.' He set off again. Wearily, Afra picked up the food bag and shifted Lucky again so that he was perched on her hip, his arms and legs wrapped around her body.

'Only a little further,' Mwape went on. 'There is a small hillside to go down, and at the bottom there is a stream, with some trees near them. We can sleep there tonight. It is not so cold. A little, maybe, but you have your things in your bag, and I have my jacket. And you can make milk for Lucky from the stream.'

Afra felt strength flow into her as Mwape outlined this plan.

'No, he should drink bottled water,' she said,

in a firmer voice. 'He's only a baby. He might get sick.'

'He is an animal!' said Mwape impatiently. 'Think what chimpanzees drink in the forest. From rivers and pools. Rainwater on the ground. And we need the water ourselves. Do you want to get dysentery? I do not.'

She knew he was being sensible, but it galled her to admit it.

'How far is it exactly to Sokomuntu? Will we get there tomorrow?'

'Tomorrow!' She could sense that he was staring at her. 'It is forty kilometres, at least, to Sokomuntu!'

'Forty?' Her heart had plummeted again. 'I didn't – Are you sure? It's that far?'

'Yes. This is a real expedition now. A secret mission. We have to travel at night, sleep in the day, live off the land . . .'

He was James Bond again.

'What do you mean, live off the land?' she said sharply.

'We will gather fruits from here and there, snare some wild animals perhaps, or catch fishes. It is how the commandos are trained.'

'Mwape, we haven't got time to catch fish, and hunt, and all that stuff.' Afra's voice had risen too high and she lowered it. Houses might be just behind the thorn fences and clumps of grass that edged the track, and people might be inside them, noticing the voices of strangers, wondering who could be out there, so late at night, speaking English.

'No, you are right,' said Mwape, his voice sobering down again, and Afra had to admit that he was nice about it when she cut him down to size. 'There will be no time for hunting. But we will manage fine. Look how clever we have been already.'

The ground was beginning to slope downwards, and in the moonlight Afra could see the glint of water. She felt suddenly that she had to rest, that nothing, not wild hyenas, or drunken soldiers, or pursuing policemen, could goad her into going any further tonight. She half-slid down the slope to the stream and followed Mwape across it, balancing on a couple of stepping stones that protruded blackly from the silvery water.

'Over there, I think,' Mwape said, pointing through the darkness.

'Yes, I can see them. Lots of trees,' said Afra.

She stumbled towards them, reached the first one and sank down onto the dry ground. Mwape dropped down beside her.

'Eh, this is a fine place!' he said, pleased with himself. 'Water, nice trees overhead, you could live here for ever.'

Afra suddenly thought of the place she should have been in tonight: a cosy lodge in the middle of a game park, a tasty dinner on a proper table, Minette being funny and elegant at the same time.

I'm sorry Minette, she said in her head. Please, please don't worry too much. I'll be all right. Really I will. This is just something I have to do.

She pushed the thought away, and began to delve into one of the food bags. She drew out a bread roll and sank her teeth into it. It was dry, but it tasted delicious. She swallowed, and tore off another hunk. Then she opened the tin of sardines. She had never much liked the strongly flavoured, oily little fish, but tonight they tasted wonderful.

Lucky was still wrapped round her, and her gentle efforts to dislodge him had only made him cling to her more desperately. But now that she was eating, she felt him sit up and lean back, as if he was trying to watch her through the darkness. Then she felt his small hand tugging at hers, and his fingers, trying to prise her roll away.

'Lucky, no! It's mine. I'm eating this. Anyway, I don't know if bread's good for chimps.'

'Give me his bottle,' said Mwape. 'I'll fill it from the stream, and you can mix up some more milk for him.'

Afra fished in her bag, pulled out the bottle and gave it to him reluctantly.

'How do you know it's not a sewer down there?' she said. 'I mean, he could catch typhoid, or anything. Monkeys get cholera and typhoid just like we do.'

'It's OK.' Mwape stood up. 'I have seen women from the farms nearby. They collect their drinking water from this stream.'

'They do?' Afra was reassured, but an unwelcome thought struck her. 'That means they'll be down here early tomorrow morning. We'd better not sleep in, Mwape, or they'll see us.'

Mwape disappeared towards the stream and came back a few moments later with a full bottle and handed it to Afra. It wasn't easy in the dark to find the milk powder in her bag, to measure out the correct amount, and tip it into the bottle without spilling it, and Lucky, who had lost interest in the bread when he had smelled the milk, didn't help at all. He began to bounce weakly up and down on his hind legs, making grunting noises.

'OK, OK, it's coming,' grumbled Afra, trying to manoeuvre the teat onto the bottle.

She managed it at last, and thrust it into Lucky's mouth. He began to suck vigorously.

'You'd never have thought,' Afra said, yawning, 'that this was the same baby who wouldn't open his mouth twelve hours ago.'

Mwape's own mouth was too full to answer. He wiped the crumbs off it, took a swig of water out of one of the bottles and handed it to Afra.

She drank deeply.

'I guess we'd better not drink this all at once,' she said sleepily. 'We have a long way to go.'

She put the bottle down carefully and lay back. The ground was hard and uneven, but she stretched out on it gratefully. If she closed her eyes, she could almost imagine that she was in a bed, and that the warm little bundle curled up against her was Wusha, her father's dog.

A moment later, she was asleep.

12

IN THE FOREST

The stars were still dancing overhead when Afra woke up. She was cold and the ground underneath felt hard. A stone was digging into her ribs, and another into her shoulder. She wondered for a moment where she was, and tried to move into a more comfortable position, disturbing Lucky, who gave a kind of squeak and cuddled down against her again.

The memory of yesterday's extraordinary events flooded in on her and she sat up abruptly, appalled by what she had done. She could see Mwape lying a little way away, huddled under his jacket, and she pulled her own closer round her, shivering with cold. She remembered everything now, the storm, the plane's emergency landing, finding Lucky, the flight to Lubumbashi, the escape from the airport.

There was a hint of greyness on the horizon. Dawn must be on its way. In a little while it would not be safe to stay here. Women would soon be coming to the stream to fetch water or to wash their clothes.

She stood up and stretched, then picked up

Lucky's bottle and started feeling her way down to the stream to refill it. Lucky started panting and hooting anxiously, scrambling after her. He patted her heels as she walked, almost tripping her up.

'Hey, you little rascal,' she said, turning round to him. 'I'm not carrying you yet. You'll be breaking my back all day, so you had just better get a little exercise before we start.'

By the time she'd filled the bottle and returned to the trees, Mwape was yawning and sitting up. Silently, morose with sleepiness, he plundered the food bags, passed her a banana and the last of the bread, and they both gulped down a little water while Lucky greedily guzzled his milk. Minute by minute, the sky was growing lighter. They bundled their warm clothes back into their bags and stood up.

Mwape led the way. He walked heavily, as if his little shoulder bag, Afra's bag and the carrier with the water bottles in it were weighing him down. He turned once to see if Afra was following him, and in the grey light she could see a scowl on his face. There was no James Bond swagger in him now.

Afra felt depressed herself. As soon as she had stood up, Lucky, who seemed much stronger this morning, jumped up, hooked his fingers into her belt and swarmed up her till he was sitting in his old place on her hip.

She laughed.

'Why, you—' she began.

Mwape turned on her.

'Don't make a noise!' he said angrily. 'Do you want people to hear us?'

'OK, I'm sorry,' she said placatingly.

She knew how he felt. She usually felt awful first thing in the morning too.

They had walked for half an hour, falling into a somnolent rhythm, before they heard the first human voices. The sound jerked Afra into instant alertness and she dived off the track into a freshly dug field. She looked round wildly. There was nowhere to hide here, and a thatched hut was only a hundred metres or so away. People might come out of it at any moment. A little further on, though, there was a giant termite mound. It towered up three metres high, turreted and crenellated like a mini castle. She dived behind it with Mwape close behind her. The voices passed on down the track and faded into the distance, but the door of the hut was creaking open now, and people were coming out. She could hear them yawning and coughing in the fresh morning air.

'What are we going to do?' she whispered to Mwape.

His face was alive and eager again, his eyes darting.

'Wait,' he mouthed at her.

Afra peeped round the mound. A woman and

a girl were going back inside the hut and she could hear the clatter of pots.

'Now!' hissed Mwape.

He was dashing across the open ground towards some trees that bordered the field. With Lucky bumping uncomfortably on her hip, Afra raced after him. They could hear more voices from the track now, children, who were laughing and calling to each other.

They're going to school, thought Afra, and she felt a pang of envy for the normality of their morning.

'Look, we can't stay on the track,' she said in a low voice to Mwape. 'There are too many people.'

He nodded.

'I have a new plan. We will walk off to the side. There are farms running along it but look, beyond the fields, there is just a kind of forest place. I think it goes on for a long way.'

She looked at him doubtfully.

'We'll get lost.'

'No. You can see, the sun is rising. It shows us the south. We will use it to guide us. Just follow me. I'll show you the way. Don't worry.'

His patronizing tone irritated her, but she had to admit he was right.

'OK,' she said, biting back a retort. 'I guess we don't have any choice.'

Luck favoured them for the first part of the

morning. They had to dodge around small farms at first, wary of dogs, scared of unexpectedly running into farmers on their way to the fields, or women going off to fetch water. Once or twice they were nearly seen, and only Mwape's quick thinking, or Afra's acute hearing saved them.

Lucky was becoming harder to handle. He drank greedily the milk Afra gave him, and it seemed to flow directly into his veins, restoring his strength. His sore foot was healing quickly too and didn't seem to bother him any more. Though he was still easily frightened, grinning and clashing his teeth with fear if he heard a dog bark, or the sound of strangers, he was clinging less tightly to Afra, and when they stopped occasionally for a rest, he would run off a little way to explore, turning over fallen pods and inspecting their insides, or pushing over small termite chimneys, delicately picking out the wriggling white grubs and putting them into his mouth.

The rests were few and far between though. Mwape, who was increasingly silent, a preoccupied frown wrinkling his forehead, said very little, and Afra was conscious only of the distance they had to cover, the pursuers who might be after them, and their meagre stock of food and water.

They had been going for several hours now. The last farm had been some while ago, and they were walking through a featureless land of spindly young acacia trees and the raw stumps of older trees that had fallen to the charcoal burners. Only a little undergrowth interrupted the monotony of the flat forest floor.

They had found what seemed to be an old track, and had been following it for half an hour, each lost in their own thoughts, when Mwape stopped suddenly and squinted up into the trees.

'What's the matter?' said Afra.

'The sun. The shadows. Which way is the south?'

She looked down at the ground and her stomach curdled. The shadows were short now, as midday approached, but something looked wrong.

She stared down, trying to calculate their position in her head.

'We're going the wrong way,' she said. 'We're going west, not south. When did you last check?'

'Not since we found this track.' Mwape sounded worried. 'I just thought – I don't know – I thought it was the right way.'

'I thought so too,' she said. 'I guess I stopped thinking about it at all.'

She slumped down to the ground. She was hot and tired and thirsty. They had a long way to go and they were lost. She wanted to cry.

This was a crazy, stupid, mad idea, she thought. However did I get myself mixed up in this mess? How could I have trusted this fantasy freak?

Mwape put the bags down, and sat down on a tree stump.

'We should rest a little while and eat something. There are still two bananas and a few biscuits.'

'Eat?' snapped Afra. 'And what do we do when our food's all gone? We could be lost in this forest for days. Weeks, even. We might never find our way out at all.'

Mwape was already drinking deeply from one of the water bottles.

'We cannot be lost for long,' he said, wiping his mouth. 'We will go south again, and we will reach the river. It is there. We cannot mistake it. And when I get to my mother's house, aiee! She will cook her best food for me. It is so good, what she does.'

I'm not going to your mother's house, thought Afra, and the people at Sokomuntu might not give me anything to eat at all.

She eyed him resentfully and reached for the water bottle. She was so thirsty she wanted to drain it to the bottom, but she forced herself to leave enough to make up another feed for Lucky. Mwape groped into the food carrier and pulled out the last two bananas. He gave one to her.

'We cannot go on all day without food,' he said. 'Why should we keep carrying it and not eat it when we have it?'

He peeled his banana and began to eat. Lucky watched him curiously.

Afra peeled her banana too and took a bite. Mwape was right, she supposed. There was no point in not eating the food they had. She bit into the sweet yellow flesh, then looked down as Lucky laid a hand on her leg and turned pleading eyes up to her.

'Oh, OK,' she said, and broke off a piece of banana for him. He grabbed it and turned his back on her, hunching his little black shoulders as he nibbled at the fruit, then, liking it, thrust the whole piece into his mouth and turned to beg for more.

'No,' said Afra, eating the last mouthful. 'Sorry, Lucky. I need to eat too if I'm going to carry you.'

She threw away the peel and Lucky scampered after it, picked it up and began to scrape at the soft inside with one black fingernail, sniffing the pith and licking it off. Then he lost interest in it and ran off.

Afra sat back against a tree. The water and the banana had made her feel better, and she took without a second thought the handful of crumbling biscuits Mwape was offering her.

'What's that you found, Lucky?' she said, idly watching the little chimp, who had picked up a round brown fruit and was carrying it back to her. She took it from him and showed it to Mwape.

'What's this?'

He slapped his leg delightedly.

'A monkey apple! They are good to eat. There, you see? I was right. We can live off the land.'

She tossed it to him. He caught it and pounded it on a stone a few times to crack the hard shell. Lucky, who had seemed unsure of Mwape up till now, crept forward to watch. The shell splintered, and Mwape pulled out some soft brown flesh and put it into his mouth.

'Nice,' he said, extracting some more.

Lucky was standing in front of him, bouncing on his feet and making grunting noises.

Mwape laughed.

'You found it, so it is yours,' he said, and he gave it to Lucky, who ran a few metres away and began to pull at the fruit with his fingers, lifting the shell to his mouth and sucking at it, making a funnel with his long flexible lips.

'He's getting stronger,' said Afra, half-pleased, half-apprehensive. 'We'd never be able to hide him in a box now.'

Lucky threw away the empty fruit shell and came cautiously back towards Mwape. He sat in front of him, looking at him for a while, then shuffled closer and began to untie Mwape's shoelaces.

'Hey!' said Mwape. 'You can't do that!'

He pulled his feet back. Lucky advanced, and tried again. He found an end to the lace and pulled it, managing to undo it. Mwape crossed his legs, tucking his feet firmly beneath his knees. Lucky looked up at him out of his large brown eyes, ran off and came back a moment later with another monkey apple. He held it up to Mwape.

'He is making friends with me,' said Mwape, looking pleased.

Lucky had chased off after a third fruit when he stopped suddenly and let out a scream of alarm. Afra was on her feet in a moment, running towards him. She saw what he was looking at and stopped, reeling back as if from a blow.

The head of a cobra had risen up out of a drift of dead leaves. Its blue-grey body, two metres long, snaked away along the ground, and its hood was up, ready to strike.

13

THE LONG ROAD TO ZAMBIA

Before Afra could move, Lucky had leaped away and was climbing the nearest sapling. Afra backed off slowly and the cobra, no doubt the most alarmed of them all, coiled round on itself and streaked off, disappearing at lightning speed into a hole under the root of a tree stump.

Shaken, Afra looked up at Lucky. In his still-weakened state he hadn't ventured far up the tree. He was screaming 'Huuu!' and 'Wraa!' and swaying backwards and forwards, making the bush of leaves at the top of the sapling rattle.

Afra managed to laugh.

'It's OK, Lucky. You don't have to scare me off too. It's gone. You can come down now.'

'What happened? Why is he upset?' said Mwape.

'Didn't you see the snake?' Afra looked round at him, surprised. 'A cobra, with its hood up.'

'Where? I will kill it!' Mwape leaped to his feet.

'No! Why? It didn't hurt us. Leave it alone,' said Afra, but before she could say more, Lucky made an unexpected flying leap onto her back, almost knocking her over.

'Wow!' said Afra, getting her breath back. 'OK, let's get out of here.'

'Where do you want to go?' said Mwape. 'It's midday now. The sun is right overhead and there are no shadows. I don't know which way south is. Do you?'

'Oh. No. I guess not.' Afra hesitated. 'But I just want to get away from that snake hole.'

She began to walk towards a clearer patch of ground.

'I don't believe in this snake of yours,' she heard Mwape grumble, but he followed her, and they stopped a little way further on.

Afra checked the ground carefully before she dared to sit down again, but there was no movement anywhere on the forest floor, except for a line of ants, who were marching purposefully along a little groove that their tiny feet had made in the hard-baked earth.

She sat down and rested her back against a tree. The snake had made Lucky restless. He didn't want to settle beside her, but ran on a little way and climbed into the fork of a bigger tree, one of the few left standing by the charcoal burners, settling himself in a fork of the trunk.

'Aren't you scared, Mwape?' Afra said suddenly, looking across at Mwape, who had sat down a little way away.

'Scared? Of snakes?' He looked at her scornfully.

'Not of snakes. Of what happens if they catch us.'

'No. If they catch us, my father will make them release us.' He sounded unconvincingly confident.

'Of what your dad's going to say then. Isn't he going to be totally, completely mad at you? Mine is.'

He frowned, picked up a twig, and began to bend it between his fingers.

'Perhaps he will not even notice I am not there,' he said. 'If he does, perhaps he will not care.'

'Doesn't he talk to you much, then?'

'Talk to me?' Mwape's voice was rich with scorn. 'When that woman is there, never! He never talks to me. He does not think about me at all.'

'My dad used to be a bit like that,' said Afra, 'not thinking about me, I mean, but I kind of found out that he did think about me. A lot really. He just doesn't show it much.'

'How did you find out?' said Mwape, interested in spite of himself.

'Different things happened. I ran off in the night once. And then another time I got bitten by a dog with rabies. After that I felt OK with him. Now I just kind of force him. You know, if he looks right through me, I go, "Hello? Is anyone there? It's me! I'm here! Your darling daughter! Say something, why don't you." It makes him laugh. It usually works.'

Mwape smiled reluctantly.

'I think you are very good at getting the things you want.' There was admiration in his voice. 'Like you have made me take you to Zambia.'

Afra sat up.

'I made you take me to Zambia? Hey, whose idea was this crazy journey, anyway?'

Mwape put his hands up.

'OK, OK, it was mine, but you would have done something even worse if I had not suggested it.'

Afra looked at him shrewdly.

'I'm just your excuse, Mwape. Go on, admit it. You want to think you're doing me a favour, and saving poor little Lucky, but really you just want to get your dad all wound up to check out if he cares.'

Mwape snapped the stick and threw the pieces away.

'So what if you are right?' he said.

'So nothing. I'd probably do the same if I was you. I hope it works. I bet it does. I'll tell him, if I ever see him, what a great job you're doing. I'd never have got this far without you. I'd still be hiding round the back of the airport with one poor hungry little chimp.'

Mwape laughed. His face looked younger, its expression more natural than it had been before.

'Why are you so worried about getting Lucky to Sokomuntu?' he said suddenly. 'It's like he was your own baby or something, but he's only a chimpanzee.'

'I know.'

Their new closeness made her think about his question properly.

'I guess I've always loved animals. When I was little, looking after an animal, it was like having a baby sister or something. I was lonely, maybe. And then the more you know animals, the more you feel—' She stopped, not knowing how to put it. 'Well, when animals love you, and trust you, they become your real, real friends. You have to love them back. You can't break their trust, because you can't explain things to them. They just see how you are, and that makes you know yourself. And you feel really special for them.'

She sat up. She was absorbed with her thoughts now, trying to work things out clearly.

'Animals are so interesting, and they're all totally different, like people, with personalities, even little animals, and birds. And they do things for reasons. It's kind of a challenge, getting into their heads to see how they think and what they want. Anyway, they have a *right* to live.' She was growing indignant now and her voice was rising. 'And who says humans have a *right* to kill wild animals, and just wipe them out? Eat them? Buy them and sell them? Shove them into cages? Destroy their forests?'

She stopped, flushed and angry.

'Are you going to be a vet when you grow up then?' said Mwape, but before she could answer he put up a hand to stop her. 'Quick! Someone's coming!'

Afra jumped up. She could hear voices approaching, and feet rustling through the leaves. She ran up to Lucky's tree and stretched up her arms.

'Lucky! Quick! Jump!'

The little chimp seemed to hear the urgency in her voice and leaped down on top of her. He coiled his arms round her neck and clung on to her tightly, burying his head like an anxious child under her chin.

'Where can I hide?' she whispered to Mwape.

'Over there. Look, behind those bushes.'

Trying to run noiselessly over the ground was impossible. The forest floor was littered with dead sticks and pods that snapped underfoot, but behind her she could hear Mwape, moving around noisily to cover her retreat, and whistling between his teeth.

'Hello, my sisters!' she heard him call out in a cheerful voice.

Peering between the leaves, she saw two girls in bright headscarves who were carrying bundles of sticks on their backs. They saw Mwape, and stopped in their tracks.

'What are you doing here? Are you lost?' they said.

'Yes, yes! That's it. I am lost,' said Mwape. 'I am trying to go south, to cross over the river into Zambia.'

'I will come with you,' giggled one of the girls. 'Zambia's better than Congo. There are no militia there. It is peaceful in Zambia.'

'You have come too far away from the track,' the other girl said. 'You should go back that way, and you will find the track again. It will take you to the border post.'

'The border post? There are police there?'

'Yes, of course. To check your papers.'

'Well, sister.' Mwape lowered his voice confidingly, and Afra could see, by the way their heads were bent towards him, that he was charming them. 'The truth is, I have lost my papers. It is better for me not to go to a border post at all. If I go on through this forest, will I come to Zambia?'

'You will.' Both girls nodded enthusiastically. 'But don't lose yourself. There are a few farms this way, but not so many. It is easy to get lost. Even us, we come here every day for our firewood, but we lose ourselves sometimes.'

'And do you see many snakes, like the big cobra I saw just now?' said Mwape, in a conversational tone.

'A cobra?' they shrieked. 'Where?'

'Just around here,' Mwape said casually.

The girls took off, their heavy bundles of sticks bouncing on their backs.

'Goodbye, brother,' they called out over their shoulders, pointing through the forest. 'Go that way.'

Afra came out when their noise had died away.

'Mwape, forget being an action man,' she said. 'You should go on the stage. You're a terrific actor.'

They both laughed, then picked up their bags and went on.

There were few laughs to come for the rest of that day. They walked on and on, hot and thirsty, working out the direction from the shadows and making corrections by their watches as, above the trees, the sun moved slowly round to the west.

There was only a little water left in the last bottle by the time dusk fell, and Afra's lips were cracked and dry.

'How far now do you think?' she said at last, after neither of them had spoken for nearly an hour. 'Get off me, Lucky. I need a rest. My back's breaking.'

'We are halfway, maybe,' Mwape said doubt-fully. 'I do not think we are more than that.'

'Halfway! But we have no water! And it's nearly dark!' Afra was trying to control the tremor in her voice.

'We must sleep in the forest tonight,' Mwape

said dully, 'and go on tomorrow. I want to lie down and sleep right now.'

'But we can't!' Afra felt panicky. 'There was that cobra, and there might be leopards.' She shook her head, trying to clear it. 'Look, in one way it's more dangerous, but I guess all round it's better for us to be near people. At least we'd have a chance to get some water. There was a footpath back there. Did you see it?'

Mwape nodded wearily.

'Let's go back and follow it and see if it takes us to a village. I can hide with Lucky, and you can go and look around for water. No one suspects a boy on his own. Those girls didn't, anyway.'

Mwape didn't bother to answer. He simply turned and began to walk back the way they'd come, towards the footpath.

It was miserable, having to retrace their steps, and scary to think of being near people again, but Afra knew they had no choice. Without water, they couldn't carry on. Alone in the forest at night, they might not even survive.

The track was nearer than she had thought. They had walked down it in silence for no more than a kilometre, when some way away through the trees they saw a column of smoke rising from beside a hut. It looked so welcoming, so ordinary and human, so full of the promise of food and water, shelter, and the company of people, that

Afra had to restrain herself from running towards it.

'OK,' she said. 'This is it. I'll wait here, look, behind these trees. You go and scout around.'

Afra had left a few inches in the last bottle of water to make up another feed for Lucky. She found a good place just off the footpath, settled herself down with her bag beside her and took out the tin of milk powder. She opened it and set it down on the ground alongside the feeding bottle, and turned to pick up the bottle of water, but Lucky, who had been watching with interest, lunged forwards, snatched up the bottle and scampered off with it.

'No!' called out Afra, keeping her voice low, afraid of the people near the hut. 'Lucky, bring it back. Come on now! I want to make your milk!'

Lucky, much stronger now than the pathetic, dehydrated little creature of yesterday, ran up a tree and sat, just out of reach, as if he was inviting Afra to join in the game.

'Come *down*!' hissed Afra, exasperated. 'Are you crazy?'

Lucky's lips were round the top of the bottle now. The lid was still on, but he was nibbling and sucking at it, working it loose.

Afra felt her temper flare. She had never dealt

with such a child-like animal before, never encountered what seemed like almost human, wilful naughtiness.

'Lucky, do you hear me? Come here at once. Give me that bottle,' she wanted to shout in the commanding voice her father used whenever she roused his anger. But Lucky was an animal, not a child. She couldn't reason with him. She could only threaten and frighten him, and that would get her nowhere.

She sat down, defeated, under the tree, and felt, like a shower of rain, the last few precious drops of water landing in her hair. Lucky had levered the top off the bottle, and had tipped the whole lot out.

Afra sat, her dripping head in her hands, beaten. This had been one of the roughest days of her whole life. After a night on the bare ground, she had walked for endless miles with almost no food and water, hot, exhausted and frequently frightened, with a heavy load to carry. Her feet were sore, her heels blistered, and she had a bad gash on one arm where a thorn bush had ripped her. Her thirst was as insistent as a toothache.

All day she had taken strength and comfort from the affectionate burden in her arms, from Lucky's evident need for her, his trust, the sweetness of his physical presence. She had almost imagined that she was his mother and he was her child. She had even assumed, somewhere, in the back of her mind, that he understood what she was doing for him, the risks she was running and the sacrifices she was making, and that he was grateful. Now she felt illogically disappointed.

That's so stupid, she told herself severely. You must never think that animals are people. I'm a girl. He's a chimpanzee. End of story.

She looked up at him. Lucky was playing with the empty bottle, banging it on a branch, then turning it round in his hands, fascinated by the way the golden light of the sun, low in the sky now, glanced off the shiny corrugated plastic. She looked away again. The sight of the empty bottle and the thought of the drink she could have had, was making her pointlessly, stupidly angry.

She didn't hear Lucky climb down from the tree, and she didn't see him creep quietly up behind her. She turned only when a glint of moving metal caught the corner of her eye. Lucky, delighting in his lovely new game, had grabbed the open tin of milk powder. He was sticking his fingers into it, then sniffing and licking them.

Afra, galvanized into action, shot her hand out to grab the tin, but Lucky was too quick for her. He tore off, holding the tin upside down, and the milk powder tumbled out, rising in puffy white clouds as it hit the ground.

Afra wanted to burst into tears. She wanted to get up, pick up her bag and march across to the hut, give herself up, go back to Lubumbashi, face

Mrs Hamble and all the angry people hunting for her there, and leave Lucky alone in the forest to look after himself. She suddenly remembered an expression her aunt had used. 'As mischievous as a cartload of monkeys.'

'That's you,' she said out loud, pointing to Lucky. 'Aunt Tidey meant *you*.'

Lucky lost interest in the tin. He dropped it and raced back towards her, flinging himself with abandon into her lap and lifting his face trustingly to hers. Her anger ebbed away.

'Oh Lucky,' she said. 'Lucky.'

'Afra, are you there?'

Mwape was calling to her through the trees. He ran up, breathless and beaming.

'It is all arranged! Come on. Let's go!'

She looked up at him, shocked at the noise he was making.

'Did you get some water?'

'No, later. Listen, there is a man here. He has a jeep. He is driving south now, across the border. He will take us with him!'

'Along the road? But they'll see Lucky and stop us. They'll take him away!'

'No. He is going by a back way. He too does not wish to see the police. He had a problem with the militia men. They beat him.' He paused. 'There is only one difficulty.'

'What?'

'We have to pay him.'

'How much?'

'Thirty dollars.'

Afra gasped.

'Thirty? But I have only twenty left. That's all my holiday and emergency money.'

He shrugged.

'It is better to pay and go with him. Give him your twenty, and when I reach my mother she will give him the rest. Otherwise, we must sleep out again tonight and walk all day tomorrow.'

Reluctantly, she nodded.

'Did you tell him about Lucky?'

'Yes. He says that is OK, but you have to put a lead on him. He doesn't want a chimpanzee jumping about on the steering wheel.'

She was about to object, but thought better of it.

'OK,' she said.

Half an hour earlier, she would have angrily refused to tie Lucky to anything, but now that she had experienced his newly energized playfulness she knew she would have to restrain him.

A small group of people was clustered round the jeep, which stood, its engine already idling, outside the hut. Afra approached nervously. She felt as if she had become a wild animal herself, instinctively avoiding people, afraid of roads and houses and cars and anything that smelt of humanity. She was braced to turn and flee.

Lucky had begun to hug her close as soon as

he had heard new voices, and looking down she could see that his lips were pulled back in a grimace of fear. The last embers of her irritation with him vanished, and she murmured to him soothingly.

The man at the jeep's wheel was short and stocky, with one eye half-closed by a puffy swelling. It gave his face a villainous expression. He hardly looked at Lucky, but jerked his head towards the back of the jeep.

'Get in,' he said, throwing a rope into the back seat. 'Tie the monkey up.'

Afra climbed in after Mwape, talking soothingly to Lucky who seemed terrified of the car. There was a woman in the front seat already. She looked sullen and nervous.

This is crazy, Afra thought. We don't know who these people are. They could be kidnappers, or murderers, or anything.

Her heart thumped uncomfortably as she gently eased the rope round Lucky's neck and held the end of it in her hands. Lucky seemed intrigued rather than put out. He sniffed at the rope and fingered it, then he settled back against her, looking over her protecting arms at the driver and the woman in front, out of large scared eyes.

Slowly, Afra's fright receded. The man and woman were conversing in a language she couldn't understand, but they sounded calm, and uninterested in their passengers. Once or twice, Mwape joined in with a comment and a laugh.

'What are they talking about?' she whispered to him. 'What language is this?'

'It is Bemba, my mother's language,' Mwape said happily. 'They are telling me about the militia soldiers and their foolishness. They are eager to return to Zambia.'

It was getting dark. New fears crowded in on Afra. She wasn't afraid of being murdered now, but she was scared of the coming night, of wild animals, and hunger, and thirst, and sleeping out in the open again.

'Where are they going? Where will they drop us?' she asked Mwape.

To her surprise, the driver answered in English.

'You are going to Sokomuntu? With the chimp?'

'Yes.'

'I can leave you near there. There is a river just before you reach that place. There is no bridge but you can find a boat to take you across.'

'Thanks,' said Afra. 'Will we get there tonight? Are we nearly at the border yet?'

'We have crossed the border,' the man said. 'We are in Zambia now.'

Mwape let out a crow of triumph.

'Tonight I will see my mother!' he cried.

Afra felt a jolt of dismay.

'Aren't you coming to Sokomuntu with me?'

'No.' Mwape was using his knees as drums, beating out a dance rhythm. 'You will go there on your own. I am going on to Chingola. My mother will be so surprised when she sees me!'

Shoots of anxiety were burgeoning in Afra's head. She hadn't expected this. She had imagined that she and Mwape would arrive at the chimp refuge together, that Mwape would be there to give her moral support and back up her strange story.

'But I can't speak Bemba,' she said. 'What if they don't understand me?'

Mwape laughed.

'They are white people at Sokomuntu,' he said. 'They speak English.'

'Oh.'

Afra felt more nervous than ever. White people would see things from her father's point of view. They would be shocked and disapproving. Telephone wires would start to hum. She would be scolded and interrogated and Prof would arrive like an avenging angel. She sat in silence, gazing out into the darkness.

At last the car pulled up. Afra could see the dull gleam of water through the trees, and lights some way beyond it.

'Sokomuntu is there,' the man said. 'When you have crossed the river, you must walk up the hill. That is all.'

'Cross the river,' Afra repeated uncertainly.

'You will find a boat,' the man said impatiently. He was obviously anxious to go on. 'But be careful. There are crocodiles here. Big ones.'

Mwape helped her out with her bag and waited while she fished in her money belt, pulled out her last dollar bills and gave them to the man. He jumped back into the car.

'I'm sorry I can't come to Sokomuntu with you. This is my best chance, with these people, to get to Chingola and find my mother. I am just hoping she will be there.'

'She will be,' said Afra, trying to sound confident. 'Thank you for everything, Mwape. You've been brilliant.'

Mwape stuck his head out the window.

'Goodbye,' he said. 'Have very good luck.'

Then he wound his window up and the car drove away. Afra, her bag on the ground beside her and the little chimp clinging fearfully to her neck, stood watching, alone and frightened, as it disappeared down the rough, deserted track into the night.

15

A FEARFUL CROSSING

The night, and the terrors it might contain, crowded in on Afra. Her eyes, peering into the darkness, could see nothing except for the water some way away, and her ears were straining to interpret a medley of sounds. The rustling in the undergrowth could just as well be a rootling porcupine as a nest of snakes. The splash from the river was probably a diving rat or a jumping fish. There was no need to assume it was a crocodile.

Something brushed her shoulder, and her body, taut with fear, responded of its own accord. She grabbed her bag and was crashing blindly through the trees towards the river before she realized that it had only been a dead leaf, falling from the tree overhead.

She halted on the river bank and stood panting and shivering, waiting for her panic to subside.

The quarter moon was up now and it made a silvery path across the water. Afra tried to assess the river's width. It was hard to tell in this strange light, but she guessed it was about twenty metres from one bank to the other. A twig floating on the surface showed her that the current was sluggish. It wouldn't be too hard to cross if only she could find a boat.

She looked up- and downstream. Thick, high-crowned trees sprouted up on both sides of the water, their dense leaves black against the indigo sky. There was no sign of human habitation, no light, no flickering blaze from a friendly fire. But now she could hear something. The sound was so low and regular that her ears hadn't registered it before, but there it was, quite definitely, the mechanical thrum of a generator. It was coming from the hilltop on the far side of the river.

It's from Sokomuntu. It must be, she thought.

A splash from upstream made her turn her head. Something was approaching, coming towards her on the water. The moonlight picked up an unearthly shimmer of white, and for one eerie moment her scalp prickled as her hair stood on end, but then she saw that the white was a shirt on the back of a man. He was standing up in a canoe, poling it deftly through the water. As he lifted up the pole and plunged it down again, the moon caught the drips and sent them scattering in a diamond shower.

He turned sharply into the bank not thirty metres from where Afra and Lucky stood in rigid silence, and Afra could hear the bottom of the boat grate on the river bottom. Then the man picked something up and slung it over his shoulder. As he jumped out onto the bank, Afra saw that the thing was a dead animal, some kind of antelope or buck.

He's a poacher, she thought, shivering.

She had half-decided to call out to him and ask him to take her across the river, but now she didn't dare. Lucky might seem like a valuable prize to him, and in this dark, quiet place it would be easy for him to snatch the little chimp away.

She waited until the man's footsteps had faded completely away, then crept down to the boat. It was a simple dugout canoe. She had been in one before, out at sea, with a boy called Hussein, and she knew how unsteady they could be.

Gingerly, she stepped into it, trying to keep her balance in spite of the chimp sitting on her shoulders. She grunted with satisfaction as she saw that the man had left the pole lying in it. She looked up and down the river again. Everything was quiet.

'You'll have to get off me, Lucky,' she whispered. 'I can't get this thing over the river with you on my back.'

'Wraa! Wraa!' Lucky cried out fearfully.

'What is it?' murmured Afra. 'Can you smell something? Is it the water? Are you scared of water, Lucky? Is that it?'

She had to peel him away from her, and managed to resist his frantic efforts to climb up into her arms again.

'Here, take my scarf,' she said, pulling it out of

a side pocket of her bag. 'Please, oh please, Lucky, don't play me up now.'

Lucky grabbed the scarf and huddled down beside Afra's bag in the bottom of the boat, moving his feet fastidiously away from a puddle.

The pole was long and horribly difficult to manage. Afra managed to push the canoe off from the bank quite easily, and it slid away, out into the moonlit water, but as she pulled the pole back it hit the side of the canoe, which rocked dangerously. For a moment, Afra teetered, desperately trying to regain her balance.

No, no! *No!* she was shouting in her head.

The water was so dark and still it looked almost oily. Nothing moved except for a log, floating slowly and silently downstream towards her. Afra had only just regained her balance and was about to try lifting the pole again when the log bumped against the canoe. She sat down suddenly, afraid of losing her balance again, and stared at the thing with shudders of horror. Was that round protuberance an eye? And what was that bump on the end of it? Was it a knot in a piece of wood, or could it be a reptilian nostril?

Suppressing the urge to scream, Afra took the pole and poked it at the object. Wood met wood. The thing was not a crocodile. It submerged briefly, then resurfaced, and floated on its way.

Afra watched it go, then roused herself. She was tired now, so tired she had entered a strange state, a kind of dream world in which nothing made much sense, or mattered any more.

She tried to concentrate, to pull herself together.

I've got to do this, she told herself, or we'll float down this river for ever and ever until we meet the sea.

She lifted the pole and tried again. It hit the bottom and she gave it a good shove. The canoe wobbled horribly, but it moved a little further towards the opposite bank.

'It's all right, Lucky.' Afra was speaking out loud without meaning to. 'We're nearly there. Listen. That's the generator. That's Sokomuntu. I bet it is. And if it isn't, if it *isn't* – Well, then, we're stuck. That's all. You and me. We're stuck.'

She was acting automatically, lifting the pole and pushing it against the river bed. Lifting and pushing. Lifting and pushing.

'I don't know what we'll do,' she went on, mumbling her words. 'I don't have a single cent left. We'll have to trust people, that's all. Go to people and trust them to help us. But I'm not going to let you go, Lucky, not just to any old person. Only if you like it, then I'd let you stay.'

She could hardly believe it when the boat bumped on the river bed a metre or so away from the opposite side. She scanned the bank anxiously. Were those empty shadows, or could they be crocodile lairs? She half-shut her eyes, straining to see through the dark.

Lucky, now that the canoe had stopped moving, dared to leave the security of Afra's bag. He hooked one strong hand into the waistband of her trousers and a second later had scrambled back up into her arms.

'That wasn't so bad,' she said. 'We made it across there all right. I said we would. Stop that wriggling now, do you hear me? OK. We have to move. Listen here, all you crocodiles. We're not for eating, Lucky and me. Did you get that? OK, Lucky, here goes!'

She picked up her bag, jumped out of the canoe and raced past the shadowy bushes. Nothing stirred. She looked back at the canoe, which, like a log of wood itself, was floating away from the bank and drifting gently downstream.

I don't care, she thought a little guiltily. The guy was a poacher. He deserves to lose his boat.

She looked up. The generator sounded nearer now.

'Come on,' she said to Lucky. 'If this is Soko-muntu that's where we are. If it's not, that's where we're not.'

She was aware of sounding incoherent, but she didn't care. Light-headed with hunger and exhaustion, she walked on up the path, her arms cracking under the weight of Lucky and her bag, hardly aware of the soreness of her feet.

She rounded a corner and saw a light ahead of

her. It was streaming out of an open doorway, and inside she could see people moving about.

'You want to know something, Lucky?' she said dreamily, hardly knowing now if she was speaking out loud, or if the words were running around inside her head. 'In this life, when it comes down to it, you're on your own. People love you. I guess your mom did, and I do, but in the end you have to manage. You have to do stuff on your own.'

She had walked into the circle of light and was standing looking in at the door. A woman, short and stocky, wearing a worn T-shirt and old trousers, looked up, saw her, and gasped with surprise.

'Pete!' she called out. 'Pete, come here. There's a couple of kids at the door, one human and one chimpanzee.'

Afterwards, Afra couldn't really remember what had happened next. She stumbled into the brightly lit room, and Lucky climbed round her shoulders so that he was peering out from behind her back. Then she was sitting down on a chair, and the woman she had first seen was sitting at a table opposite her, next to a man who looked like Father Christmas, an elderly man, whose face was framed in a white circle of beard and hair.

'Gordon Bennett,' the woman said. 'Will you look at these two? Half-dead, by the looks of it.

Come on, Pete, let's get her some tea and something to eat. She looks starved. Food first. Talk afterwards. And that baby needs milk, if I'm not mistaken.'

It wasn't until Afra had consumed a huge plateful of tasty stew, had drunk what seemed like litres of water, and had given a still timid Lucky two full bottles of milk that her wits began to recover. When they did, strange feelings, a mixture of relief and joy, dread and an awful loneliness welled up inside her, and she put her head down on the table and was engulfed in a tidal wave of tears.

She felt Lucky hugging her close, and sensed that the woman was coming near her too. Then there was an angry scream from Lucky, and a sudden scuffle, and the woman stepped back. Afra stopped crying and looked up, suspicious and alarmed.

'It's all right,' the woman said. 'I wanted to give you a tissue to blow your nose on, but your young friend didn't like it. He gave me a little bite. Nothing serious. He knows you're upset. He's just trying to protect you.'

Afra stopped crying and laughed shakily.

'I'm sorry,' she said. 'You must think I'm kind of crazy. You see, I—'

'It's all right,' the woman said calmly. 'You don't have to talk yet. It looks like you've travelled a heck of a way, and you're tired, and you've been frightened. Oh, and I think you could do with a long night's sleep in a proper bed. How does that sound?'

'I can't leave Lucky,' Afra said quickly. 'You won't want him in a bedroom. We can sleep outside. We did last night.'

The woman laughed.

'Look,' she said, 'I've had more chimps in my spare bedroom than human beings. What's his name, by the way?'

'I call him Lucky,' said Afra. 'And I'm Afra. Afra Tovey.'

'I'm Jean,' the woman said. 'And this old curmudgeon's Pete. Welcome to Sokomuntu, Afra.'

16

SOKOMUNTU

Lucky woke Afra. He had slept in a tight ball of black hair, pressed hard against her. She had felt, once or twice during the long night, the warmth of his tough little body, curled into her back. She had heard, too, through the mists of sleep, the crackle of a radio from the sitting room next door, but she had drifted off again immediately into a medley of confused dreams.

She opened her eyes at last to find Lucky sitting on the pillow grooming her hair. He was gently parting the strands and examining her scalp, smacking his lips and emitting occasional grunts of contentment. As soon as he saw that she was awake, he lay on his back and presented his tummy to her, wanting to be groomed too.

She extended a sleepy hand, and began to pull wisps of dead grass out of his hair.

'I could have slept for ever, you little rascal,' she said lovingly.

She stretched, and winced as she felt the stiffness in her arms and legs.

'I feel as if someone beat me all over with a baseball bat,' she groaned. 'How about you,

Lucky? I guess you must feel kind of weird today too.'

The door opened and Jean appeared. Her face was flushed, and she was drying her hands on a towel.

'Chasing Patty,' she said succinctly. 'She was teasing the dog.'

Afra sat up.

'Who's Patty?'

'Another new arrival. She's taking time to settle in. She was found in a box going round the luggage carousel at Lusaka airport. In a terrible state, she was.'

Afra stared at her.

'You mean she's a chimp too?'

Jean laughed.

'Yes, of course.' She sat down on the end of Afra's bed. She was holding a feeding bottle full of milk in her hand, and Lucky began eyeing it greedily. Jean carefully didn't look at him.

'I expect you're wondering . . .' Afra began tentatively, and stopped.

'Well, yes. I am, rather,' said Jean. 'Take your time. Begin at the beginning.'

It took a few false starts, but once Afra began, her story poured out. As she told it, she watched Jean's eyebrows rise further and further in astonishment.

'That's quite a story,' Jean said, when at last Afra had fallen silent. 'I can hardly believe it.'

'I know.' Afra wriggled her blistered toes nervously under the blanket. 'I can hardly believe it myself.'

Lucky had been creeping cautiously across the bed towards the bottle, which Jean had put down casually beside her. He darted forward suddenly and picked it up. Then he sat back, and stuck the teat into his mouth.

'He doesn't know about holding it up,' Afra said. 'I usually hold it for him.'

Still keeping her eyes averted, Jean had already put a gentle finger under the end of the bottle and was tilting it up so that the milk could flow into Lucky's mouth. Without seeming to notice what he was doing, Lucky put up his hand and closed it over Jean's. Afra watched, trying to control a spurt of jealousy.

'The reason why I believe your story, all of it,' Jean went on calmly, as though nothing had happened, 'is that everyone in Africa seems to be looking for you. I made a few radio calls last night, and as soon as I mentioned your name, the airwaves started humming. You wouldn't believe the number of people who've been on to me this morning.'

'Oh.' Afra looked at her warily. 'Was one of them a man called Professor Tovey, by any chance?'

'Your dad? You'd better believe it. Sounded madder than a jar full of hornets. I told him he'd have to cool it if he wanted to come to Sokomuntu.'

'You did?'

Afra looked at Jean with awe.

'Then there was the Hamble woman. Half-demented, she was.'

'Do you know her, then? Mrs Hamble, I mean?' said Afra.

'Petunia Hamble? Of course I do. Known her for years.'

'Petunia?' Afra couldn't help giggling. 'That's not really her name, is it?'

'Yes. Do you wonder she never lets anyone call her by her Christian name? Poor old thing. She was in such a state I thought she'd burst right out into hysterics when she heard you were here, safe and sound.'

Afra screwed her nose up. She knew she ought to feel bad about Mrs Hamble, but she couldn't.

'Treated you like a baby, did she?' said Jean. 'I suppose she drove you witless. Treats everyone like that, Petunia does. Got no kids of her own. Good-hearted though. She's a really fine person.' She frowned sharply. 'You've upset everyone. I hope you're sorry.'

Afra took a deep breath.

'Well, I'm sorry everyone's upset, but I'm not sorry I did it. I had to give Lucky a chance. Running off with him was the only way I could think of.'

Jean looked down at Lucky. He had finished his bottle and was patting her hand, as if asking for more. A lump rose in Afra's throat. Maybe she wasn't special to him, after all. Maybe any kind person, who would give him milk, would do as a replacement parent. She looked up to see that Jean's expression had softened.

'No, I suppose you didn't have any choice. I'd have done the same, if I'd been you, except that I wouldn't have had the courage. You're quite a girl, Afra Tovey. Mind you, I'm glad you're not my daughter.'

Afra smiled shyly at her.

'Have you got any? Daughters, I mean?' she said.

'No. Twin boys. But I've got seventy chimps here. Seventy-one, if you count Lucky. That is why you brought him here, isn't it? You want him to stay with us?'

Afra was watching Lucky who, confident now in Jean's company, was turning a somersault on the bed. She swallowed, then looked up at Jean.

'I guess so.'

Jean stood up.

'We'd better get on with it then.'

'Get on with what?'

'Introducing him to his new family. It can take days if they don't accept him straight off. Get your clothes on and have some breakfast.' She went to the door and turned back. 'They get under your skin, don't they?' she went on, her voice so understanding that tears welled in Afra's eyes. 'If it's any comfort, I think we get under theirs, too. Lucky doesn't understand what you did for him, of course, but he's never going to forget you, as long as he lives.'

It was bright morning outside. The tree-fringed compound that surrounded the small house was empty, except for a couple of dogs, a big goose, and a tribe of chickens, who were pecking around in the dust. A young man was wheeling a barrow full of battered fruit across to a storeroom.

'*Mwapoleni*,' he called out to her.

She waved, not understanding the Bemba greeting. The man disappeared. There was no sign of Jean or Pete.

Then she heard Jean's voice coming from behind a group of low outhouses.

'Come down here, you idiot!' she was yelling. 'If you think I'm going to let you sit up there and starve yourself to death, you've got another think coming!'

Afra walked cautiously towards the sound, and came upon Jean, who was standing below a tree, waving a piece of meat in the air. Above her, a great bird was sitting hunched on the top branch.

'A snake eagle,' Jean explained. 'Broke his wing weeks ago. I patched him up and got him back to flying again, but he's not hunting properly yet.

Can't feed himself, and doesn't want to take food from me any more. Obstinate little terror, he is. Makes me go down on my bended knee.'

She whirled the meat again. With a sudden whirr of his great wings, the snake eagle plunged, snatched the meat from her hand and retreated with it to his tree.

'And about time too,' Jean said, looking up at him triumphantly. 'There. You'll do now.'

Afra looked at Jean's strong bronzed face and her shabby old clothes and felt an almost painful shock of recognition. Jean was the living embodiment of her own secret dream. Jean's life was the life she had always wanted. For years she had had a vague kind of vision in her mind, a picture of a remote corner of Africa, and of herself at the centre of a place like this, surrounded by needy animals, creatures that she had rescued, that she would care for, devoting herself to them night and day, nursing them back to health and life. She was looking at what she had always imagined to be her own ideal future. Unexpectedly, the reality was somehow uncomfortable.

Jean saw the stunned expression on her face.

'What's the matter with you?' she said. 'Seen a ghost?'

Maybe I have, Afra thought. The ghost of my future.

There was a sudden riotous outbreak of screams and hoots from one of the outhouses.

Lucky, who had followed Afra outside and was tentatively exploring a discarded orange peel, screamed too, and leaped up into her arms.

'That'll be Patrick,' said Jean. 'He's taken the little ones out for their morning walk in the forest, and now he's giving them their lunch. Come on. It's now or never.'

Afra felt Lucky's little body quiver with excitement and apprehension as she followed Jean down a path between some old sheds to a fenced-in yard. The man she'd seen before was standing by the mesh fence, putting fruits into the out-stretched hands of five or six small chimpanzees.

'These are the youngest ones,' said Jean. 'Up to four years old. Lucky'll go in with them if they accept him. He'll be their new brother.'

Afra felt like a mother taking her child to his first day at school. The young chimps were jostling good-naturedly for Patrick's attention, grabbing at the fruit, then tucking it away in their hand-like feet, or into their armpits, or in the crook of their elbows, and reaching out for more.

Lucky, hanging on grimly to Afra, watched them nervously.

The last fruit disappeared and the chimps ran off into the corners of the yard to eat it.

'Go on,' said Jean. 'Take him up to the netting.'

Nervously, Afra approached. For a few moments, none of the chimps took any notice of her, then one small female looked up and began to make grunting noises. Slowly, she ambled up to the wire and put a hand through it, reaching out to touch Lucky's shoulder. At once, Lucky began to make lip-smacking noises and he put up his hands and began to gently groom the hair on the other chimp's arm.

'That's a good start,' Jean said quietly. 'She's a real little mother, Leni is. She's been here for over a year. Rescued from poachers who had shot her mother out from under her. She was half-starved when she arrived. Look at that! She's accepting him already.'

One by one the other chimps were approaching the mesh. They put out their hands to touch Lucky, and he waited quietly, letting them feel him, his tension subsiding and his confidence growing.

'Would you believe it?' said Jean. 'This bit takes days sometimes. Weeks even. Your little guy's passing all his tests with flying colours. Look, I've got things to do. Stay with him, Afra. Give him an hour or so. I'll be back soon.'

She left, calling out to Patrick, and Afra stood quietly, holding Lucky, watching the little chimps. They were in a playful mood. One dangled himself by one arm from a strut in the fence, scratching his tummy with his free hand, till another came up and tugged at his foot. Then they took off in a wild chasing game, grunting and shrieking. Ignoring them, two others sat together in a peaceful huddle, grooming each other with concentrated attention. From time to time, one would break off and amble over to the wire, where Leni still sat. She had pushed both hands through the mesh and was holding Lucky's, letting go sometimes to scratch her head, or to scrabble at something on the ground, before turning back to him. Slowly, they were making friends.

Soon, Afra began to tell the chimps apart. She could see that each one was an individual.

Lucky's not going to like you much, she thought, watching one boisterous youngster race up and thump another on the back. The first chimp turned and took him in a flying tackle and they began to play-wrestle amicably on the ground. Or maybe he will. I don't know. It's all boys' stuff. I guess he'll be OK.

By the time Jean came back, Lucky had livened up. He had pushed Afra away and was climbing around on the mesh as if he wanted to get inside with the others.

'That's quick work,' said Jean, looking at him appraisingly. 'I don't usually put a new one in as fast as this. He wants to go, though, you can see that. OK. Let's do it. In you go, Lucky.'

A moment later, Lucky was in the yard with the other chimpanzees. He sat for a moment near the door, looking almost shy, then Leni came up and put her arm round his back. Together, they moved off, Lucky walking on his knuckles, Leni with one arm still round his back, and disappeared through a hole in the wall at the far end.

He's gone already, Afra thought. I've lost him.

She felt a dreadful emptiness.

'He won't stay in this cage thing for ever will he?' she said. 'It's kind of small.'

'No.' Jean shook her head. 'They only stay here when they're little. Patrick takes them out every morning into the bush, to get them used to being out in the open. Once they're big enough we integrate them slowly with the adult groups, who have their own huge area of bush and trees. We don't see much of them after that. We still have to feed them, of course, but they're more or less on their own then. In their own society.'

Afra hardly heard her. She was still staring unhappily at the small door through which Lucky had disappeared.

Jean touched her arm.

'Let him be,' she said. 'Give him a chance to settle in. We'll come back later and see how he's getting on.'

'OK.' Afra turned reluctantly to go. Her arms felt weightless and empty. The future looked strangely and suddenly bleak.

A car appeared as if from nowhere, turning in through the gates of the compound in a flurry of noise and dust.

'Who's this?' said Jean, puzzled. 'Pete got back

a while ago, and I'm not expecting anyone else today.'

The car stopped and a tall man with a shock of unruly, straw-coloured hair leaped out. Afra stepped back, a look of horror on her face.

'Do you know him?' said Jean.

'Yes,' said Afra. 'It's my father. It's Prof.'

17

A SECOND-BEST ENDING

Afra had expected her father to be ablaze with anger. She had infuriated him many times in the past, had disobeyed him, run away from him and driven him wild with anxiety. Every time she had felt the whiplash of his rage. Never, though, in all her thirteen years, had she done anything as awful as this.

She saw her adventure suddenly from his point of view. She had disappeared in a war-torn country, a place bristling with drunken militiamen and armed bandits, vanishing without trace, leaving no message, no clue, no explanation. He must have thought she'd been kidnapped, at the very least. He'd probably imagined that she'd been murdered. He must have been crazy with worry.

She crossed her fingers behind her back and walked towards him, expecting a blast of rage to scorch the very ground she stood on. But Prof looked pale and shaken. He simply opened his arms and took her into a crushing embrace.

'Oh honey,' was all he said.

After a while she stepped back and looked at

him. There was an awful, painful heaviness in his face.

'Prof,' she began. 'I'm sorry. I'm really, really sorry. I guess you were kind of worried about me, but—'

'I've been asking myself over and over,' Prof interrupted. 'What did I do? Were you angry because I didn't come with you? Was it Minette? I know you felt bad when I started dating her, but I thought you two had become good friends. I know I'm a lousy father. I guess you were trying to tell me . . .'

His voice petered out.

Afra stared at him, aghast. This was worse than anger, worse even than the contempt he had sometimes heaped upon her.

'Prof! No!' she cried. 'It was nothing to do with you. Of course I like Minette, you know I do. I was really excited about going to Luangwa. It was just that something happened. Didn't Jean tell you? I found a baby chimp. I had to rescue him.'

She looked round to see if Jean was still there, but Jean had tactfully disappeared.

Prof sighed.

'She said something about a chimp. Of course, I guessed an animal would be involved somewhere in all this, but I knew it had to be more than that.'

'Oh, it is. It was.' Afra saw the stricken look in his face and stretched up to kiss him swiftly on the cheek. 'No, nothing to do with you, Daddy. Honestly. I told you, I'm really, truly sorry I got you all so worried. It wasn't you. It was what I saw. What was going on at Mumbasa.'

'I knew you'd landed there,' said Prof, puzzled. 'Mrs Hamble called me. If ever I heard a demented woman . . . But what happened there? Did you see fighting? I thought that area wasn't affected by the civil war. Oh sweetheart, I hoped you'd never be involved with all that kind of thing. After your mother and I came through those ghastly years in Ethiopia, we promised each other that our child would never have to witness any kind of war.'

She took his arm and shook it gently.

'It was nothing to do with fighting, Prof. At least, not between people. It's what's happening in the forest. To the chimps and gorillas.'

He had been staring into the distance, but now he focused on her again.

'What do you mean?'

She took a deep breath.

'They're cutting down the forest, Prof. The loggers. From Europe.'

'I know. It's a shame, but there's nothing much we can do about it. It's been going on for years.'

She shook her head vehemently.

'It's not just the trees. Hunters go in after the loggers. They're shooting all the animals they can

168

find. They're killing all the chimps and gorillas, to sell for *meat*. For people to *eat*!'

He frowned.

'But they're protected species. It's illegal.'

She snorted.

'They don't care. They're just making money out of it, as quickly as they can. Lucky – he's my chimp – his mom was killed. I saw her body. It was so horrible, Prof. It was strapped on to the back of a log on this huge truck. And Lucky was in a box, being teased by the kids, terrified, half-starving. You would have rescued him. You would have done the same as me.'

He was about to answer when Jean appeared.

'I'm taking the little chimps out into the forest now,' she said. 'Do you want to come?'

'Lucky's going out too?' said Afra.

'Of course.'

Afra grabbed Prof's hand.

'You'll see him,' she said, pulling him towards the little chimps' quarters. 'Come and meet him.'

The baby chimps, feverishly excited at the prospect of their daily outing, were hooting and shrieking in a deafening cacophony of sound. Jean had hardly opened the door when they hurtled out, six black tornadoes of hairy energy. Lucky emerged last. He moved nervously, unsure of what was happening, but then he saw Afra, and hurled himself at her, scrambling up into her arms, flinging his own round her and bouncing with excitement. She dropped her face into the soft skin of his short neck.

'Hi, little guy,' she managed to say, through the lump in her throat. 'I thought you'd forgotten me already.'

She turned to show him to Prof, but Prof was reeling under the impact of more juvenile chimp enthusiasm. One small creature was already sitting on his shoulder, and another was climbing up his leg.

'Hey!' he was laughing. 'Watch out! Don't *do* that! Mind my spectacles!'

Jean pulled the chimps off him, as easily as if she was picking plums.

'They're supposed to walk,' she said. 'Lazy little tykes. Their mothers would have shaken them off long ago.'

'Hear that, Lucky?' said Afra fondly. 'I carried you all day yesterday. You can manage on your own today.'

Gently, she put him down on the ground and began to walk after Jean. She felt his small hand tug pleadingly at her shorts and she had to harden her heart.

'He's bound to be a little nervous,' Jean called back to her. 'It's only natural. He's the new boy here.'

Leni had been running ahead, on all fours, but she turned round suddenly and stopped. She waited until Afra and Lucky came up to her, then hooked her arm round Lucky and walked along-side him.

'Buddy-walking,' Jean said with satisfaction. 'Ninety-eight point six per cent human, they are. You can tell just by watching them.'

She was leading them away from the river, into a tract of acacia forest. Afra looked round. It had been like this yesterday. She and Mwape had walked for miles and miles, hour after hour, through trees like these, making detours round similar giant termite hills, scuffling over identical dead leaves and pods. She shivered. Yesterday, the forest had seemed a hostile, maze-like place, full of hidden dangers. Today it was beautiful, a world of shifting light and shade, of birdsong and friendliness.

She remembered the cobra and turned to tell Prof about it, then bit back the words. He'd had enough to worry about. She'd leave the snake out of it.

Jean stopped at last in a small clearing. The chimps seemed to know the routine. At once they began to play. Two chased each other up into a tree. Another one, finding the growth of a soft termite chimney that was no taller than himself, began to pull at it, working away until he had rocked it off its base and knocked it right over. He sat down beside it, looking with fascination at the scurrying insects inside.

Leni sat down beside Prof, and stared intently

up at him. Then she climbed onto his lap, and cautiously folding down the top of his ear, began to investigate the skin behind it.

Prof laughed.

'You're tickling me!' he said.

He began to tickle Leni back. She rolled over and over, kicking her legs in the air, writhing in soundless paroxysms of laughter.

Afra, watching them, realized she had lost sight of Lucky. She looked round, anxious, then saw that he had climbed the tree after the other two. Loud rustlings and the cracking of breaking branches came from overhead.

'What are they doing?' she asked Jean.

'Making nests to rest in,' said Jean. 'Like their mothers did.'

Leni tired of the tickling game and ran off.

'Where did Lucky go?' said Prof.

'He's up there, with the others,' said Afra, pointing up into the tree.

'This is a happy ending, I suppose,' said Prof.

Afra said nothing. She was seeing Lucky's mother again, the body on the truck, Maurice and Dieter, the pygmy with the gun. She shook her head.

'Not really,' she said. 'It's a second-best ending. The best would be for him to be at home with his family. For none of this to have happened at all. Or for him to have found his big sisters and to have gone on living safely with them.'

She picked up a couple of stones and jiggled them about in her hands. She hesitated for a moment, glancing at Jean. She wanted to speak frankly, but didn't want to hurt Jean's feelings, but Jean's face was so calm and open that it gave her courage.

'I got a shock this morning,' she said to Jean, 'when I saw you with that snake eagle. You're what I always wanted to be. A person running an animal sanctuary, I mean. Rescuing animals, and living with them.'

Jean shook her head.

'Be like me?' she said. 'Are you kidding? You have to be crazy to do all this.'

'No.' Afra shook her head too. 'You're not crazy. It's totally brilliant here. Sokomuntu's one of the best places I've ever been to in my whole life. But it's not enough. It's – it's like a plaster on a really deep wound, that needs, oh, I don't know, stitching, and operations, and skin grafts and stuff. You can only help a bit here, just rescue a few of the victims. I bet there's another Lucky, right now, sitting in a box in Mumbasa, and those horrible men are driving around with another dead chimp on the back of their truck.'

'You're right,' said Jean, 'of course. We're not solving the problem here. Just picking up a few of the pieces.'

'*Well*,' Afra shook the hair out of her eyes. 'I had a sort of revelation this morning. I know

now. I've decided what I'm going to do with the rest of my life. I'm going to fight them. All of them. The loggers, the hunters, the businessmen, the pet smugglers. And come to think of it, the trawlers that are killing off the fish, and the poachers, and – and – I don't know what to call them. Exploiters! Yes, that's the word for them all. Exploiters.'

'Are you now?' said Jean, a hint of laughter in her voice. 'And how are you going to do that?'

Afra threw the pebbles away. She sat up straight, her eyes shining.

'I don't know yet, but I'll probably have to hold meetings, and write letters, and get people to demonstrate, and tell people who buy wood from Africa about what's happening to the animals in the forest. I'm going to make a fuss. A great big *fuss*.'

The laughter went from Jean's face and she nodded.

'Good for you, Afra. We need people like you. Looks like you'll be good at it. You know how to get everyone in a fuss already.'

Prof was staring at Afra as if he had never seen her before.

'What's the matter?' she asked him.

'It's a weird thing,' he said, 'really quite alarming, when you say goodbye to your child one day, and a couple of days later, when you meet her again, she's turned into a young woman.'

*

The little chimps were tired when at last they returned to their yard. Lucky ambled inside without a backward glance at Afra and reluctantly she followed Prof and Jean towards the house.

'I wanted to ask you, Prof,' she said, with a nervous little laugh, 'but I didn't dare. Have you contacted Minette? Was she very upset with me?'

'Yes, I did. And yes, she was,' Prof said. 'Worried, rather than upset. Frantic, actually. But she knows you're OK now. I said I'd bring you on to Luangwa tomorrow, if you were in a fit state to travel.' He looked down at her appraisingly. 'You look fine to me. We're leaving early. Around eight.'

'You mean you're still going to let me go to Luangwa, after all this?' Afra said incredulously. 'Thanks, Prof. I didn't expect it. I thought I'd be on bread and water for weeks.'

'Who said anything about a fancy diet?' said Prof. 'For all I know, Minette's going to feed you to the lions down there.'

'I'm going to buy her an enormous present,' said Afra enthusiastically, 'just to say sorry. At least, I would, if I had any money. Prof, you couldn't lend me—'

She broke off. Pete had come out of the house and was signalling to them.

'Boy called Mwape calling for you, Afra,' he said. 'On the radio.'

Afra hurried inside and put the earphones on. Mwape's voice crackled down the line.

'Afra? Are you OK? Over.'

'Yes. I got here all right. Lucky's staying on here. It's all fine. I'm going to Luangwa tomorrow. Did you find your mom? Over.'

'Yes. She is a bit sick. I am so glad I came. I am going to stay here and look after her. I telephoned my dad. You were right, what you said. He was really worried about me.'

A burst of static interrupted him and his voice began to fade.

'Write to me in Nairobi, Mwape!' Afra shouted. 'Come and see me!'

But Mwape had gone. She turned back to see Prof, Jean and Pete regarding her curiously.

'Mwape, eh?' said Pete. 'Your boyfriend, I suppose. Dozens of 'em, all over Africa, I shouldn't wonder.'

She blushed.

'Don't listen to him,' said Jean. 'Come and have some tea.'

'How's that little fellow of yours settling in then?' said Pete, stirring sugar into a big mug of tea. 'Thought he looked a bit peaky when I went round there this morning. Cheered up, though, when I gave him my banana.'

Afra beamed at him.

'You're not a curmudgeon at all,' she said. 'You're an old softie.'

'Shh, don't tell him that,' said Jean. 'You know what men are like. It'll go straight to his head.'

Early the next morning, before anyone else was stirring, Afra crept out of bed and went to the baby chimps' yard. A go-away bird, perched among the purple flowers of a jacaranda tree, set up a startled call, and the deep booming cry of an eagle answered it. The adult chimps, a long way away in their forested enclosure, were restless too this morning. Rising alarm hoots sounded out from among the trees, ending in ear-splitting shrieks which died away again almost immediately.

The adults' unrest had disturbed the babies too. They had tumbled out of their sleeping house, and were clambering around on the mesh fencing in their yard. Lucky was busily investigating a beetle in the dust when Afra arrived, but he jumped up at once as she called to him and ran to her, grunting.

She knelt down beside the netting and took hold of his hand. He sat quietly, letting her keep it in his, then pushed his other arm through the netting and began gently smacking his lips, asking to be groomed. She began to work on his forearm, pulling off pieces of sticky pith from the fruit he'd been eating the day before. He was relaxing now, lolling against the mesh, his eyes fixed languorously on her face.

Leni ran up. Jealously, she pushed out her own arm, demanding attention. Afra complied, combing out burrs and pieces of dead broken leaf. Leni relaxed too, leaning against Lucky as comfortably and familiarly as if they had been friends for years.

Then Lucky stretched out his arm and pulled Afra's head towards him, grunting invitingly. She let him draw it up to the mesh, and bent her neck as he began to groom her. She shut her eyes, feeling the gentle tugs as he pulled back her curls to inspect her scalp, touching it delicately with the tips of his hard little fingers.

She stayed like that for a long time, until at last she heard sounds, human sounds, coming from the house behind her. She didn't want anyone to find her here. Reluctantly, she pulled Lucky's hands away from her head, held them for a moment, then dropped them.

'Goodbye,' she whispered.

There was nothing else to say. She stood up and walked away, the sweetness of his smell still in her nostrils, the softness of his touch lingering in her hair like a blessing.

Elizabeth Laird
Wild Things 10:
LION PRIDE

Joseph sat bolt upright in bed, woken by a strange noise.
Every hair stood up on the back of his neck. A deadly
predator was prowling right outside the house. . .

Joseph's family live in constant danger when a hungry lion
starts preying on farms in their remote valley. When his
cousin is badly mauled, Joseph and a team of trackers must
set out on a desperate hunt. Closing in on the lion in its
rocky lair, they know a snarling attack could come at any
second. . .

WILD THINGS titles
available from Macmillan

The prices shown below are correct at the time of going to press. However, Macmillan Publishers reserve the right to show new retail prices on covers which may differ from those previously advertised.

ELIZABETH LAIRD

1. Leopard Trail	0 330 37148 7	£2.99
2. Baboon Rock	0 330 37149 5	£2.99
3. Elephant Thunder	0 330 37150 9	£2.99
4. Rhino Fire	0 330 37151 7	£2.99
5. Red Wolf	0 330 37152 5	£2.99
6. Zebra Storm	0 330 37153 3	£2.99
7. Parrot Rescue	0 330 39301 4	£2.99
8. Turtle Reef	0 330 39302 2	£2.99

All Macmillan titles can be ordered at your local bookshop or are available by post from:

Book Service by Post
PO Box 29, Douglas, Isle of Man IM99 1BQ

Credit cards accepted. For details:
Telephone: 01624 675137
Fax: 01624 670923
E-mail: bookshop@enterprise.net

Free postage and packing in the UK.
Overseas customers: add £1 per book (paperback)
and £3 per book (hardback).